A Fresh Start
at
Well Cottage

By Sally E. Morgan

This book is dedicated to;

Lillie Florence Mitchell 1913-1943

The Canadian crew members of Wellington
Bomber R1465

A Fresh Start at Well Cottage

Chapter 1

Amy

A decrepit navy blue Land Rover, exhaust spewing filthy grey fumes, pulled to a halt at the bottom of the hill. An elderly man with two dogs emerged from the driver's door. My pulse quickened as both hounds ducked under the field gate and raced towards me. A whistle pierced the air; one animal went to heel. The other, a black and white mutt, kept running. My stomach clenched and I ran too. After being bitten as a child, dogs terrify me.

Making for the stile, I told myself not to act scared, that dogs always knew. The animal was much faster than me, its panting breath at my back in seconds. It overtook me and stopped in front of my only way out. Trapped, I squealed in horror as a whistle peeped repeatedly. Shouts of 'Hamburger, heel. Hammy come here,' sounded across the field.

Eyes squeezed shut, every muscle in my body tensed as I waited for teeth to tear my flesh; nothing. I opened an eye and exhaled. The dog sat on its haunches, head to one side, ears cocked. I allowed myself to open the other eye and relaxed a little, then inspected the odd-looking creature in front of me; its coat wavy, almost curly.

Everything about the animal's behaviour; his intelligent hazel eyes soft and tail wagging furiously, told me it was ridiculous to be scared. He wanted to make friends and be patted.

The owner of the Land Rover puffed up the hill towards us, calling to the dog.

'Sorry about that, Miss,' the man said, as he pulled off his grubby flat cap. 'He's a friendly chappie, young Hamburger. Doesn't mean any harm. Got a tad more training required. Dare say he thought you were a sheep and needed rounding up in that cream fleecy jacket.'

'Hamburger?'

'Yes, the daft creature is crazy for burgers.' He leant, scratched behind the dog's ear and said, 'Any kind will do, Burger King, Birds Eye, but a McDonald's is his favourite.'

Then he asked, 'Don't suppose you can point out Rooks Row Farm? I'm delivering Hammy there. He's their new sheepdog. Their old dog is half blind and can't herd sheep any longer.'

'You've stopped too soon. Rooks Row is next left. Not far, the turning is in 200 yards and opposite my cottage, the one with a green door.'

The man clearly liked to chat. 'I warned Raymond Giles that Hammy's not fully trained or pure bred. He's the only one ready to work and able to manage with simple orders, "Come Bye" and "Away" for right and left. He's less sure with his whistle commands.'

Both dogs capered beside to me, demanding attention. Hamburger curled himself up on top of my trainers, his eyes gazed into mine. He seemed taken with my feet, kept sniffing them. I couldn't move until he did, not without kicking him off, anyway.

'Hamburger has a wavy coat. That must be unusual for a sheepdog?' I asked.

'Aye, his mother took a liking to a labradoodle, the other pups in the litter look the same as any other Border Collie. Hamburger has always been... different. He's clever and affectionate, so I trained him the same as the rest. A grand fella, he will make the grade. I'll be off to take him to his new home. Thanks for the directions. Come on, lads.' He touched his cap, and they headed down the hill.

At Well Cottage I pushed open the squeaky green garden gate, made a mental note to oil the hinges later, then bent to pull up a weed from the red brick path. Aunty Jen was lending me her cottage in return for my looking after it while she visited my cousin in New Zealand.

Mum impressed on me that I had to mow the lawns and keep everything immaculate. Jen could have rented out the pretty cottage for thousands instead of allowing me to house sit.

After Alan and I sold up and split the sale proceeds of our Bristol flat, I'd been homeless, with only a minuscule cash deposit, four mid century chairs, a

3

table and sideboard in my mother's garage to my name. The loan of the house came as a godsend.

I'd resolved to use the time in Talwern to change my life; no more cocktails with the girls, catching the bus, and pizza Deliveroos. I would exercise and run on home working days instead of paying a fortune at the gym, then pay occasional visits to the cute yoga studio I'd spotted in a restored barn. The money saved would go towards the deposit on a bigger, nicer flat; one to call my own. So what, it might be lonely? It was only for six months until Aunt Jen returned and gave me a chance to rethink my future; a future without a man. I'd given up everything for Alan, friends, the career I loved, and for what? Betrayal, I determined to go cold turkey give up on men.

More happened in Talwern village than I expected, with a thriving local history society, watercolour classes and Zumba in the arts and craft village hall. The only thing I'm more afraid of than dogs, is water, so the sailing club on the nearby lake was entirely out.

A community run village shop and cafe operated near the school. I'd volunteered for a half day a week there, hoping to get to know people. My first shift was on Wednesday morning. I wondered about attending the harvest supper in October, but discounted the WI meetings. It would be another decade or two before I was ready for that.

Up by six on Wednesday, with a bowl of strawberry granola and a cup of steaming coffee beside me on the desk I looked out onto the front garden.

Grimacing, I worked my way through dozens of emails that had arrived overnight from our Australian office. This was followed by a Zoom meeting with the comms manager in Melbourne at seven. Late afternoon in Oz is early morning in Wales. As a lark, I've always preferred early starts. I planned to work for three hours, grab a quick shower and reach the village shop for their ten till one shift, then work the rest of my hours later in the day.

I arrived promptly at the pleasant shop, shelves full of interesting local products, like fennel and apple sausages, lavender honey along with useful basics, milk, eggs and similar. I'd completed an induction day with the enthusiastic young manager the previous week, but the shop till appeared not to remember. Every time entered more than one item, the electronic till refused to play. At least it meant I got to know Linda and Gwen, the other volunteers, faster than expected.

'It doesn't like me,' I wailed after yet another customer was kept waiting for their change.

Gwen laughed and smoothed her neat grey bob. 'It does that to every new volunteer. Don't worry. Tell you what, the veg stall could do with a clear out and clean. Try that and I'll take over till duties.'

I served a woman about my age next, who'd come in with a Yorkshire terrier and stayed for a coffee in the cafe. Her dog was unduly interested in the vegetables. It ran off with a small swede, then brought it back to my feet, and nudged it toward me expectantly.

I could only giggle and tell him, 'It's not a ball.'

His owner caught sight of his antics. 'Oh, Wilf, what am I to do with him?' she asked. 'That swede is ruined. I'll pay for it but give me another bigger one. I'll make potch, with a pound of the shop's pork and apple sausages for supper.'

'What ever is potch?'I asked.

Oh, mashed swede and potato. The potato takes a little of the bitterness away from the swede; my husband likes it fried up and crusty next day. It's like bubble and squeak or, I guess, what they call hash browns in the States.

I nodded. 'I'll have to try it. Shall I throw the swede for him?'

'Only if you want to be bothered constantly until I leave,' she laughed. 'I'm Verity James, Vee, by the way and guess you are Jenny Well Cottage's niece.'

I smiled back at her. 'I am. How did you know?'

'This is a small village. Fresh faces, especially young, pretty ones with blonde hair are big news. I live a few doors down the road from you. Why don't you pop round for a coffee? How does Monday sound? It's The Oaks.'

'I'd love to. I'm not the only new resident in the village, though. Yesterday Rooks Row Farm got a new one too.'

Gwen and Linda's heads turned.

'Rooks Row? Surely you haven't been there?' asked Linda. 'No-one much calls there.'

'I met a man delivering a sheepdog, and made the dog's acquaintance. It was very friendly.'

'That's more than you can say for that family,' Gwen said, as her lips compressed into a hard line.

Linda's eyes warned Verity and me not to say anything more.

I changed the subject. 'Those are wonderful marrows, pumpkins and squash on the stall, so lovely. I'm surprised they are only a pound each?'

It was exactly the right thing to say. The compliment distracted Gwen.

'I grew them. With the summer we've had, I've dozens going to waste. I live alone and there's only so much marrow and squash I can eat.' Verity and Linda nodded in hearty agreement. 'I'll drop off a mixed half a dozen tomorrow,' said Gwen

'My courgettes have all grown to marrow size and I've done everything imaginable with them, stuffed them, roasted them, made courgetti out of them. Ben and the kids beg not to have to eat any more,' said Verity.

'Have you heard of marrow rum? I've been wondering about making some,' Linda said. 'I saw it on YouTube. You hollow the marrow out, pour in brown sugar, raisins and wine yeast, seal it up with an airlock and wait.'

'Sounds disgusting,' groaned Verity and Gwen. I resolved to try it out.

Drew

It was a relief to pull into the farmyard at nine. I'd had meetings all day in the city, then spent four and a half hours stuck in Friday evening traffic on the M4.

Opening the kitchen door I called through, 'I'm home. Supper smells good.'

Dad limped in. 'Stew's probably dried out by now. Stop for a drink after work, did you?'

I bit a sharp retort back; he'd been alone all week. 'No, I've spent hours on the motorway. Traffic gets worse every trip.'

Dad shrugged, sighed, then said, 'I couldn't manage the drive anymore. Another thing I can't do. Me and Meg are the same, aren't we, girl? Only fit for the scrapheap.'

'You'll improve if you keep up the exercises the physio's given you.' There was a bark, followed by scratching at the kitchen door. 'New sheepdog has arrived then.'

'Aye, friendly enough creature, but not fully trained. How can I teach him when I'm like this? I can't even exercise him.'

'Don't worry, I'll take him for a long walk tomorrow. Does he have a name?'

'Breeder said he was called Hamburger, would you believe? Can't go yelling that over the fields, can we? Let's name him Jet.'

When I opened the door, a young dog bounded in, licked my hand and went to Meg's basket by the Aga. It trampled over patient Meg, turned round twice on the cushion and settled in the spot closest to the warmth.

'Goodness, that is a strange-looking collie. How much did you pay?'

'Less than half the usual; eight hundred, because he's neither pure bred nor fully trained. I trust old

Griffiths' judgement. If he says the dog will make the grade, it will. Doubt he'll be as good as our Meg. Shame I couldn't have run them together.'

He bent and stroked our old dog's head fondly. Her fur showed much grey as black these days. 'Meg would have shown him the ropes. Wouldn't you, lass?'

'Huh, the pup doesn't look worth that. Serve up supper, I'm starving.'

Next morning, I answered a dozen or so company emails. By the time I'd finished and was ready to go out, the new dog had disappeared.

Dad said, 'I saw Jet run off down the lane. I whistled and called, but he ignored me. That's a bad sign. He's got no discipline.'

'I'll put out feed for the sheep, then walk to the village and find him.'

Chapter 2

Amy

Holly Cottage looked picture perfect that first Saturday in September; whitewashed walls, diamond-leaded panes of glass in green framed windows, with a yellow rose growing over the doorway. I made a dried flower wreath of hydrangea heads for the front door, then knelt to arrange Gwen's squash and pumpkins on the doorstep. I'd started a batch of rum in the largest marrow she'd left me, earlier in the week. I'm a domestic goddess in the making, I thought. If only there was a god to come home and appreciate me.

After mowing the lawn, I jumped at the sight of a black and white shape shimmy under the garden gate. I froze, seeing the dog. I felt my heart rate quicken as it ran towards me and I gave a whimper. A warm, wet tongue licked my ankle. It was Hamburger, tail wagging, eyes soft and pleading, begging me to stroke it. I had to laugh at myself. This was a dog no one could be afraid of, and I bent to fondle the warm black fur on his head.

'OK, Hamburger, I could do with a cup of tea. Stay outside. Stay,' I said, making my voice firm. To my surprise, he did as he was told and sat, tail thumping against the paving slabs. I hide my emergency supply of a Toblerone bar and milk chocolate digestives away at the back of the cupboard to avoid temptation, so winkled out five biscuits, three for me and two for him, then headed for the wooden garden bench under Jen's gnarled russet apple tree.

I broke the biscuit into pieces and made the dog work for his treats. He'd sit and beg and I'd either give him a chunk or throw it high in the air and he'd jump to catch it. Both of his biscuits and two of mine quickly disappeared as I watched his antics.

An angry call from behind the hedge halted our fun.

'Oi, what are you doing feeding Jet? Stop spoiling my father's dog with biscuits.' A tall man with dark eyebrows glared poison over the front hedge. Flannel checked shirt collar fraying under a tatty navy blue jumper, forty or so, his dark brown hair laced with silver threads, he looked a typical farmer.

'Jet? This is Hamburger. Surely, the odd biscuit won't hurt an energetic pup?'

'Spoiling dogs always harm them. He has to work. We haven't bought him to play.'

'Hamburger's young and entitled to occasional treats,' I argued, irritated by the gorgon peering over my hedge.

'Stop calling him Hamburger. It's a stupid name. Sheepdogs need short sharp names that carry over distances.'

This bully really annoyed me. 'Maybe you need to learn to whistle. That's what he's been taught,' I countered.

Angry brown eyes, a shade darker than Hamburger's, met mine.

'Don't tell me how to manage my collie. I can't imagine you've any experience or you wouldn't be feeding him chocolate digestives. Jet heel,' he said.

11

The dog did as instructed, casting a pitiful glance back at me as he slunk away. I watched them leave and couldn't help noticing how muscular Hamburger's new owner was. What if he was more than a bully and cruel? Hamburger wouldn't stand a chance. I presumed this was the younger Giles from Rooks Row. They deserved their reputation then, and were my nearest neighbours. It surprised me that Jen hadn't given a warning.

Drew

As I marched down the lane, my annoyance grew. The last thing Dad needed with all his health problems was an unruly, half trained pup. He was barely coping with the farm as it was. It would break his heart to be forced to sell the sheep after losing the cattle. It was such bad luck that Meg's eyesight had deteriorated so badly. Damn that new dog. Wherever had it got to?

I heard Jet's bark and a woman's laughter from behind Well Cottage's hedge. I'd met the owner several times. It seemed unlike Jennifer Stuart. What was she thinking of, playing with our sheepdog without a bye or leave?

I put my head over the hedge and began to say exactly what I thought. Instead of my familiar middle-aged neighbour, a woman with honey tousled curls threw biscuits in the air for the collie. I realised I was telling off a total stranger. How embarrassing! I wasn't sure how to back pedal and apologise.

The girl refused to acknowledge any wrong doing and scolded me for changing Jet's name; what effrontery, and after feeding our dog chocolate. We can call our dog anything we choose. How dare she argue? Doesn't she know anything about dogs and the risks of theobromine poisoning? No one had spoken to me like that for years.

At least Jet came to heel when called. As we walked home up the lane, he ran ahead, but the memory of those outraged blue eyes defending him made me wince.

Dad was moping around the garden when I got back, ineffectually dead-heading geraniums.

I said, 'Let's go to Abergavenny shopping. I need to check on my place anyway, pick up some clean clothes. I'll cook there and then we come back and sleep here.'

'Have to lock Meg and Jet up in the barn or else take them,' he grumbled.

'Dad, I've barely spent any time at my house for months. They'll be fine in the barn. I have to be sure everything is OK. Aber House is low maintenance, not like Rooks Row, but even so.'

'I know, I know. Sorry. I don't mean to be such a bloody nuisance,' he said.

On Monday, I walked a quarter of a mile up the road to The Oaks; an imposing Edwardian house painted a tasteful grey and surrounded by an enormous garden my mother would love to explore.

Verity, in slate jeans and jumper, dark hair tied back in a sleek ponytail, welcomed me into a modern glass garden room. I gazed around, admiring a black baby grand piano in the corner and two long grey velvet sofas, perfect to sink into. Tall speakers filled the room with mellow jazz saxophone.

'Do you play?' I asked, gesturing at the piano.

'Not so much now. Tea or coffee?'

'Mmm, coffee, please. What a gorgeous place.'

'Isn't it wonderful? We moved here from London during COVID. Swapped our two bed flat in Camden for this. I pinch myself every morning,' she replied.

'You're not local either?'

'No, I'm from Surrey, but we love it here. The mountains, the rivers, and it's only an hour to sandy beaches. Ben has to travel to his London office two days a week and stays with his mum. We've agreed it is a small price to pay for the improved quality of life. I have taken the odd piece of work on. Not much, it's too far. Our children are four and six, so it has been great, no childcare costs, a bus takes them and collects them from school and I get plenty of time with them. How about you?'

'I work from home for three days, then spend two days in the Bristol office. I work in P.R; social media. Drive there in an hour and a bit because I start at six. When,...' I faltered, I hated saying the words out loud even after six months. I took a deep breath. 'When Alan and I split up, we sold the flat in Clifton. I had to find somewhere or move in with my parents. Aunt Jen offered to lend me Well Cottage until she gets back from New Zealand. It seemed a sensible plan. The property market is so hot right now that I can't find anywhere decent with my half of the proceeds.'

I shrugged and attempted to look positive.

14

Verity saw through me and put a consoling hand on my arm.

'Did you divorce?'

'No, the one blessing was we hadn't married. It made a clean break easy; especially for him.' I couldn't help the bitter tone in my voice.

'How long were you together?'

'Five years, but if I'm honest, the last couple were pretty rubbish. He'd found someone else. An office romance.' I shrugged again. Then tried to joke. 'I have an uncanny ability to pick cheats. I've resolved to give up men, at least for a while, and enjoy being single.'

Verity nodded, her pretty face sympathetic, then led me through to a stylish, dark green kitchen, pored boiling water into a cafetière of coffee and offered me a warm Welsh cake. I demolished three, savouring the taste of nutmeg and sultanas, and forced myself not to reach for another.

'Wow, they're great. I love griddle cakes. They don't seem to have them anywhere other than Wales.'

'I had to learn to make them. Gwen taught me.'

'Speaking of Gwen, did you see her face when you mentioned Rooks Row Farm. What's the story there?' I asked.

'No one's sure. She's from local farming stock, and they keep that sort of stuff to themselves. There are different tales; some say a milk quota argument, others, a longstanding family feud. She's related to lots of people hereabouts and is lovely, so people take her side. All I know is no one socialises with Rooks Row Farm. The father and son shop in Abergavenny, not locally.'

'Father and son?' I asked.

'Yes, the old man is in his sixties. His son is maybe forty and comes home to help his dad most weekends. Works away in construction, I think. I've only ever seen them as they drive past in a tractor or their Range Rover. They never nod, which is unusual for round here, unfriendly.'

'I met the son yesterday. He shouted at me for giving his dog a biscuit. He was horrible.'

Talk moved on, and Vee said, 'There is Zumba in the village hall tonight, you must come.It's great fun and good exercise.'

Before I knew it, I'd agreed to meet her in the hall every Monday for Zumba and to try the local rambling group on Thursday morning.

'We meet the first Thursday of the month in the Black Boar car park at ten, and car share to the start point. We usually pop in to the pub for a half afterwards,' she said. 'All ages go, mostly older, but we have a good time and the leader, Helen, takes us to fantastic spots. She knows the hills well and I get to hear all the village gossip. It's next week Amy; you must come.'

My social diary was filling fast. I'd been worried that six months in the country would be boring, but perhaps that idea was wrong.

Chapter 3

Amy

That evening I got to the village hall early, well before seven, wearing my blue Sweaty Betty yoga kit. I loved its swirly psychedelic pattern leggings, teeny matching crop-top, and matched it with a powder blue sweat top to wear until I warmed up. Groups of cheery, middle-aged and older women arrived in twos and threes. I felt uncomfortable; baggy jogging bottoms and old tee shirts were the order of the day. Overdressed, as no one wore lycra or crop-tops.

Everyone smiled curiously at me. The instructor, a lean, tanned woman in her late sixties, came over, welcomed me and checked my health. A wave of relief washed over me when Verity arrived wearing shiny emerald leggings with tight long-sleeved top, hair tied up by a bold orange ribbon. If only my wayward blonde waves could look that smart. I wished I was slim like her, not short and curvy; no amount of training or running changed my body shape.

Two teenage girls raced in, their bra tops smaller than mine. I relaxed into the warm-up session, easy. Five minutes later, a Latin American beat boomed out. Blimey, Zumba is energetic; who knew? Nothing like my flow yoga. We all panted and puffed as Helen shouted instructions. I threw my sweat top onto a chair. It was fun, but I dripped perspiration, way more than during a hot yoga session.

17

The music stopped after an hour and I gasped with relief. Gwen and Verity collapsed onto chairs next to me, drinking deeply from reusable water bottles. No one in the room except me had a plastic bottle. It was the same in my yoga studio, but there it felt OK. No one really knew me; here I felt guilty.

'Love your kit,' said Verity. 'Who makes it?' I told her, and Gwen was interested too, saying she deserved a treat and might splash out on a top online. Several of the 'girls' headed for the pub up the road, but exhausted after the session, I could only stagger home for a shower.

Helen shouted over to Verity and Gwen, 'Will you be there for the hike on Thursday?'

They nodded and Verity added, 'Amy's coming too.'

Still aching after Zumba on Monday, I had another six a.m. meeting on Thursday, catching the Melbourne office at the end of their day. It dragged on, making me rush to get ready for the Ramblers at ten. It had rained overnight, so I pushed on my short, pink Wellie boots with a cactus pattern I used for gardening and an oversized cardigan jacket. I popped a boxed M&S salad and a tangerine, along with another plastic bottle of water, into my small rucksack and headed off.

In the Boar car park, a group of a dozen men and women gathered around Helen and a map spread on a blue bonnet. I jumped out of my Honda. Everyone's eyes swivelled to my feet. Their expressions ranged from amused, through incredulous, to downright disapproving.

Helen came over, coughed, then said, 'Amy dear, if you try to walk in those, you'll have blisters the size of conkers within half a mile. They're slippery over rocky terrain, and give no support. You'll twist an ankle. Do you have nothing else?'

'My white leather trainers are in the car but, but they're new and low. I thought they'd get wet, ruined.'

Gwen interrupted. 'What size are you, Amy? Your feet look similar to mine, five and a half?'

Flushing pink, I agreed.

'I've an old pair at home, as we'll be driving past on the way you can borrow them. They aren't 100 percent waterproof. I only use them if I know it's dry, but... but they'll be better than those,' she laughed.

Helen asked, 'You do have a waterproof in your rucksack?'

My shoulders drooped lower. 'No, it is such a warm day, I didn't bother.'

'The mountains can change in an instant,' she replied and looked askance at Gwen.

'I've a spare cagoule at home,' Gwen said. 'I'll sort her out and meet you at the car park. Come on, Amy, let's go.'

Gwen's house was stone built with beautiful views over the hills. As she led me through to her kitchen, I stopped short at an arresting portrait of a young woman in her hall.

Goodness, what a lovely painting; Who is she?

'It's my great-aunt Lillie back in the 40s. I love it too. Look at that hairstyle; a Victory Roll, they called it. Her boyfriend at the time was an artist; she modelled for him and he gave it to her.'

'They didn't marry?' I asked.

'He died. He was a pilot in the RAF. Bomber crews lasted months and sometimes only weeks, before being shot down. They saved Britain, but paid a heavy price. Her family didn't approve of him, in any case. He wasn't a farmer, had no land and was over ten years older.'

'Did she find anyone else?'

Gwen replied slowly, not answering my question. 'Lillie contracted TB and died in a sanatorium outside of Cardiff the year after the war. My grandmother was devastated and the portrait of her sister became one of her most treasured possessions.'

She shook her head. 'Come on, let's find you those boots and a decent anorak.'

We returned to her immaculately clean, grey electric Mini and drove across the river and up a valley where we met our group at a lay-by.

'We're climbing the Dragon's Back today,' Gwen explained. 'It's a pull at the start, but worth it.'

She wasn't kidding; after a short section through woodland, the walk went straight up a steep bank. I was exhausted and breathless before we reached the summit.

Helen pointed around. 'Dinas was once the highest castle in England and Wales. We are standing on the site of a Norman keep, but the ditches are from the Iron Age. It guarded the valley entrance, and the route into the Kingdom of Brycheiniog. We'll follow that path up to the Beacons Way.'

How fascinating; I resolved to research Dinas online, then return to examine the hill fort on my own. I gaped at the path that snaked ahead of us; we had to climb all the way down, then back up hundreds of meters. No one else seemed perturbed, and except for Verity, they were all much older than me.

An hour later, we reached a trig point, as Helen called a halt. I flung myself onto the ground with relief. As I looked out, I realised why the walk was called the Dragon's Back. We'd climbed waves in the hills, each ridge ever higher. The view of Breconshire laid before us was stupendous.

Around me the ramblers pulled open rucksacks and thick sandwiches of wholemeal bread, thermos flasks of coffee and chunks of cake appeared. My pre-packaged M&S beetroot and feta in a plastic box and tangerine looked miserable by comparison.

Helen took pity on me. Handing over half of her wedge of fruitcake, she said, 'That salad wouldn't feed a mouse. You'll need more calories; we're not halfway through yet. Wait till we get to the top, you can see down to the River Severn.'

My feet ached and had blistered by the time we arrived back at The Boar. Laughter filled the sunlit pub garden as we toasted the walk with halves of shandy.

In Well Cottage that evening, I found not one, but three anoraks on hooks behind the pantry door, along with two pairs of sturdy Berghaus walking boots; Jen and Diane's, arranged neatly underneath the shelves; both were my size.

I sniffed as the rich scent of fermenting marrow, sultanas and brown sugar filled the room. I looked forward to tasting my rum at Christmas.

Drew

I'd a blind date on Wednesday night. I'd tried lots of dating apps, but hadn't liked any of the matches. The women never had remotely similar interests to their profile's claims; none enjoyed hill walking, or knew anything about art or design. Most came caked in make-up, looked like Barbie dolls, and constantly checked their mobiles while eating.

I decided to try the old-fashioned method and asked my married colleague and partner in the firm, Sally Gardner, whether she had any friends that might be interested in a workaholic architect with too many caring responsibilities.

She'd laughed at me. 'Drew, you're lovely, although you take life and work too seriously. If it wasn't for Andy, I would date you myself. You are a catch. Stephanie was a fool to leave you and will regret it. Promise me you won't take her back if she changes her mind.'

'Don't worry, I realise now Steph married what I was; her boss and a partner in the company. If I'd been a trainee, she wouldn't have looked at me twice.' It was hard not to sound aggrieved, but the more often I admitted it, the less it stung.

'I'm so glad you've said that, Drew. Sorry, but we all thought that when you first started seeing her.' She paused, then added, 'People talk about you and Angelique, though.'

'Angel's twenty-one, for goodness' sake, she's mentioned that her mother is the same age as I am.

22

There's nothing between us. The girl's shy; it makes her appear standoffish.'

'Good, in that case I do have a friend who might be right for you. She is recently divorced and has two children. Tracy is nice; a GP, the kind, caring sort, and grew up on a farm.'

'Sounds perfect. Could you ask if she's up for meeting some time?'

As I left, I smiled, thinking of my PA, Angelique, more commonly known in the office as the Ice Maiden, although I called her Angel.

Willowy, with smooth silver tresses, very pretty and extremely efficient. The single trainees and associates fell over themselves to please her, especially Daniel Kelly, but Angel refused to flirt. She told me once she hated the male attention her looks got her. I shook my head. I've never gone for blondes. What was Sally thinking, that I'd even consider cradle snatching my PA? I wanted a soul mate, someone with shared interests; then I wondered what my blind date would look like? Might she have deep blue eyes like that woman from Well Cottage?

When Tracy had said the only day she could make was Wednesday, my first thought was, excellent, now I'll be able to drop in on my attractive new neighbour with a bottle of wine as an apology. I shook myself; that was ridiculous. I could call in any weekend. Sally has set up a meeting with a pleasant woman, a doctor, far more suitable than a ditsy, argumentative woman from the village.

Tracy was delightful; intelligent, with stylishly cut, short dark hair, and wore subtle make up. She didn't look at her phone once over dinner. We hit it off from the moment we met at a wine bar near my office. OK, she talked a lot about her children and her ex, but we laughed too. I made my divorce sound easy. Made light of being forced to sell the Docklands flat I'd scraped and saved for in my early twenties.

'My wife leaving hit my pride and my wallet, but not my heart,' I said. 'It was a relief.' That was certainly true, I thought. It had been a blessing not to put up with Steph's demands and histrionics day in, day out.

At Tracy's insistence, we split the bill; Steph had never done that on our early dates either. As Tracy lived south of the river, she called an Uber. We kissed briefly before she climbed into the cab, and I caught the tube back to my Chiswick apartment.

I followed etiquette. Texted when I got in, saying what a great night and we should meet again soon.

Just as well, Sally checked up on me first thing on Thursday. 'Send Tracy a couple of flirty texts this week.' She looked sternly over her glasses. 'Nothing too raunchy, mind.'

I couldn't help my hurt expression. 'As if I don't know better.'

'You'd be surprised. You should read what my single friends get sent.'

Chapter 4

Amy

Friday was my office day. I left for Bristol at five and was at my desk by ten past six. The day went smoothly until the final cross-continental meeting. All hell broke loose in Melbourne. Three major clients who distributed our trendy herbal liqueurs had threatened to leave the company and recriminations flew back and fore. I tried to calm things down, but nothing worked. It culminated in two team members resigning. I soothed their manager, saying they'd reconsider by Monday and hoped I was right.

The girls in the office were off out for Friday drinks, but I was driving and couldn't join them. By seven thirty, it was already dark. Stuck in traffic, I crawled behind glowing red tail-lights for a mile along the M32, which added half an hour to the journey.

The siren call of McDonald's at the Abergavenny roundabout was insistent. Starving, I needed sustenance along with a loo break. Queueing for my McPlant burger, skinny fries and an apple pie, I noticed their all day bargain burger offer. I knew someone who'd appreciate a treat tomorrow morning.

'No mustard on that,' I said. 'No cheese either, just the burger and a bun.'

With the bulging brown paper bag on the car seat, I drove to Talwern, taunted by wafts of chips and cinnamon apple filling the car. By nine I was home. Logs crackled in the wood-burning stove and a glass of chilled Pinot dripped condensation onto the drinks mat next to my burger box. Perfect... if only I had someone to share the evening with.

After the second bite of my burger, I wasn't surprised to hear a bark outside. Someone special, with warm hazel eyes, had arrived for Friday supper. I'd read about dogs' sense of smell; they say it's between 1,000 and 10,000 times better than humans. I got up and let in my gentleman caller. His tail thumped the floor with delight. Smiling, I pulled out the second red box and put it on the hearth.

He wolfed down the burger and bun in three mouthfuls. Can a dog look ecstatic? I'd not have thought so until I moved to the county. Hamburger and Wilf were the first dogs I had ever known.

Both of us started as the door knocker sounded. Who could that be at this time of night? Hamburger hid behind the sofa. That's not like him, I thought. He's usually at my heels. I peered out of the window. It was the younger Mr Giles from Rooks Row. A sage green Range Rover blocked my gate. How did he know Hamburger was here?

I opened the front door, face flushed.

'Good evening.' The man's frame filled the small doorway.

'Oh, hello, uhh... Can I help?'

'I was driving past, and saw our new sheepdog slink under your gate. Thought I'd fetch him while I was passing... in case he was bothering you?'

'No, no, I'm here alone.'

His eyes went to the wood burner, then the empty red McDonald's box on the hearth. He took in my

26

burger in its box alongside my glass of white wine. It was obvious I was lying.

His lips twitched; he was trying not to laugh. 'You're sure you haven't seen Jet?'

'Oh, Hamburger, you mean? Yes, he's here. I thought you meant a different...'

I gave up trying to fib as Hamburger poked his nose out from behind the sofa.

'It's Friday, and I had to work late. No time to cook and knew that he loves burgers,' I gabbled. 'He came to keep me company. I didn't plan it.'

'He put his McDonald's order in before you left, I suppose? I should be glad he hasn't got a bowl of wine to go with it or I'd get no work out of him tomorrow,' came the reply. The rotter was laughing out loud.

The skin around his eyes crinkled as he smiled. He didn't look that fierce right now. Even his eyebrows were less bushy and threatening when he wasn't frowning. In fact, he looked attractive; chunky and athletic.

'I'm Andrew Giles, by the way.' He hesitated, then said, 'Drew, to my friends.' He offered me his hand to shake, 'and you're...?'

'Amy, Amy Stuart. Um, would you like a glass of wine?' I was at a loss about how to handle the change in his attitude, as I'd expected him to snap my head off, not laugh at me.

'It is late and my father won't eat until I get in. I've told him he should, but Dad insists. Says he eats alone all week and looks forward to the Friday nights I'm

27

there. I do have to go home. Another time. I'll leave the dog. I suspect he knows his way back.'

'He'll make up his own mind. Hamburger knows exactly what he wants,' I said, holding the door open. I tried not to feel abandoned as Hamburger ran off to wait by the tail-gate of the car. After buying him supper, he's off, I thought as they drove away. Like all the men in my life, he takes what he pleases and leaves. At least Hamburger can't dislike Andrew Giles that much. It sounds as if Andrew gets on with his dad, too. He looked a lot nicer when he wasn't shouting at me

On Saturday, a friend of Verity's held a birthday party in the pub in the next village, and See suggested I join them. Entering a roomful of strangers is tough, even with support; and I'd nearly bailed, but it was that or another night home alone. Vee and Ben picked me up at eight. She wore a pretty floral top and jeans, her husband a casual shirt and chinos. Ben, with sandy blonde hair, freckles and glasses, was a foil for Verity's dark good looks, more crumpled and relaxed.

For once I'd picked appropriate clothing; my favourite stone washed blue jeans clung to my curves, after a few days they got baggy, but tonight they looked good with the oatmeal sweater and pistachio silk scarf. I'd coordinated the outfit with green eyeliner the colour of the scarf and long drop earrings.

The pub was already full of people of all ages, from eighty to eight. A band, A Box of Frogs emblazoned across their drum kit, was setting up in the corner. All the usual "one, two's" of the sound check were called into the mike. Ben chatted to the guitarist, then called us over.

'Amy, this is Simon Evans. We play squash together. I've heard a lot about The Frogs. I am looking forward to hearing them at last.'

Skinny, with hair tied into a tiny ponytail and cool blue framed glasses, Simon was good looking, a cross between Harry Styles and Jon Bon Jovi; sculpted cheekbones to die for. My pulse skipped as he asked about my musical tastes. Really friendly, he regaled us with tales of the bands' gigs and mishaps.

Verity gave cool, unenthusiastic responses. When Ben fetched drinks, she whispered, 'Simon's a ladies' man. He's a bad influence on Ben. Be careful, Amy.'

I hadn't been out for ages. Glasses of wine , then Prosecco to celebrate the birthday kept coming. The band was fun; Simon played lead guitar and had all the moves, while the bass player and vocalist kept the sound together. At ten, a DJ set started, and the dance floor filled with people of all ages, Dad dancers, jivers, smoochers; everyone threw inhibitions to the wind, and disco'd to a mix of hits from the last six decades; no Ibiza or House in the Boar.

Simon tapped my shoulder. 'Dance?'

We gyrated to a few songs, and he impressed me with his moves. Afterwards, he asked, 'What did you think of the set?'

'Great, you were all fantastic.'

Thanks, which song did you like best?

'Um, maybe, Sultans of Swing?'

'Ah yes, I've a solo in that. It's a classic. Good choice. We could meet for a drink? How about in three weeks? I'm free on that Saturday. Black Boar at eight, OK?'

Self assured, it didn't occur to him I would say no. I like confident men; that's who I always go for, but Simon could have at least pretended I might have somewhere else to be.

Drew

I drove down the lane on Friday night, after calling in to Well cottage and collecting the collie, surprised by how much I'd wanted to accept that mad girl's offer of a drink. She differed from the women at work, who did what I said and were deferential; keen to butter me up, to hear about the firm's next projects. I had to admit they were bound to be. I was their boss. An internal voice whispered, she's different to Stephanie, you mean.

I sighed. Thinking about my ex made me angry. I couldn't get the memories of Steph out of my head. Thoughts about how she's deceived me went round and round, like an endlessly stuck record. She'd left for the US two years ago; furious I wouldn't leave Dad after his stroke and that I'd refused a hefty golden hello offered to join a Chicago firm. She planned we follow her dream of designing high end homes after we won the RIBA house of the year for Aber House. Planned that we become the next Scott-Brown and Venturi, a power architect couple. Trouble was, designing houses for the rich and famous wasn't my dream. Anyway, I couldn't abandon my father so soon after his stroke.

I scowled. We'd divorced a year later. The attempt at long distance marriage a failure, not least because she started a relationship with a partner of the new firm's Boston office. He'd left a wife and three children for her.

"A clean break," Steph said, but made me pay over the odds for our home outside Crickhowell. I'd bought the land for Aber House years before meeting her and designed the structure. I'd no option but to sell 'our' London flat and buy something smaller, close to my office in Chiswick, to keep Aber House.

The scales fell from my eyes on learning she had found her way into another partner's bed so quickly; months after arriving in the US. Six years earlier, I hadn't so much fallen for Stephanie as surrendered. Her campaign to please me had been ruthless, besides her face and body made resistance futile. I didn't mind, so what I wasn't in love. She was someone to come home to. I kept my normal emotional distance, was comfortable and in control and she was too.

Sleek and sophisticated, Steph wore cream cashmere all winter, a city girl to her core. She loved designing the modern interiors and did it beautifully. In Talwern, however, she moaned about the village, the mud and the Welsh weather.

I drove into Rooks Row farmyard and went in.

'Dad, I'm back,' I called. 'Come on, Jet. Go into the kitchen.'

Dad sat by the Aga, staring blankly out of the window.

'It's you, Drew. Good week?'

His voice held not a hint of interest in my reply.

'Yes, reasonable. I found Jet hanging around the woman in Well Cottage again. She'd bought him a burger, would you believe?'

'Your supper is in the bottom oven keeping warm.'

He hadn't listened to a word.

'Have you eaten?'

'Wasn't hungry. Put some in a bowl to reheat tomorrow.'

I looked at him, noticed his collar was too large for his scrawny neck; and his trousers were held up by an old belt. He'd lost stones in weight.

'No, eat with me. You're wasting away. Weren't you wearing that shirt when I left on Monday?'

'No idea,' he said.

'Dad, you can't carry on like this. I'll book an appointment to see the doctor.'

'What good will that do? Drew, accept it. I'm useless and a burden making you come here every weekend. I've lost the herd and the farm's going to wrack and ruin. We should sell up. I'll go into a home.'

'Dad, you're not sixty yet; that's not old. You barely limp. The physio said you're ninety percent recovered from the stroke. You're depressed and that's the truth of it. You need help.'

'Don't you tell me what to eat, mister fancy architect. You aren't here all week trying to keep the farm going.' He stomped out.

'Dad, you haven't eaten a thing,' I called after him.

Chapter 5

Amy

I was tired after what felt like an endless week, with only my half day in the village shop for fun. I'd a five a.m. staff meeting booked so worked from home the following Friday. Things hadn't settled in the Melbourne office. One girl withdrew her resignation, but the other was still leaving. She'd never worked hard, took long lunches and caused a lot of clients to complain. I told the CEO, who agreed and suggested I managed both the UK and Australian teams in the future and agreed a twenty percent pay rise. It was great news, but brought more responsibility, longer hours, and would mean finding time for extra morning and evening meetings with staff.

Later I rang Mum and crowed about the extra cash. 'I'll get a better mortgage and move back to Bristol,' I said.

Work canceled the final meeting of the day at short notice. I did an internet food shop, then put leftover courgette and mushroom lasagne in the oven to reheat. I had tired of "courgetti" spiralized strands and fried courgettes with everything. Gwen kept leaving mounds of the vegetable on my doorstep and I couldn't refuse. The next lot, I would dump in the compost heap, and cover with grass clippings.

It was Friday night; I'd won a promotion. I toasted myself with a glass of Pinot with supper, alone for the second Friday in a row, but lump welled in my throat and my eyes stung. I had no one to celebrate with and felt empty. My parents knew, but who else was there that actually cared? My friends from Uni thought I'd gone to the dark side with the Bristol job. They earned far less than me; academia doesn't pay. Telling them I'd got a promotion wouldn't impress, it'd seem like boasting.

I took a mouthful of lasagne, when an almighty bang sounded as the crockery on the draining board rattled. My mouth dried. Was the noise from the kitchen or pantry? What on earth could it be, a gas explosion? No, Jen didn't have gas. There was heating oil in a big green tank at the side of the house and an electric hob. Heart in my mouth, I pushed open the kitchen door; nothing. I stepped into the pantry and gazed around in horror.

Brown slime covered the walls, floor, shelves and Jen's neat rows of tins and bottles; coats and boots were all spattered with the stuff and darker blobs; sultanas. The gunk smelt of fermenting marrow. I tasted the mess gingerly; not so bad, sweet. That meant the gloop wasn't just dirty, it was sticky.

A disaster; it'd take hours to clean. I might have to paint the room. Would the smell ever subside? I'd promised Jen and Mum to care for the cottage. Tears welled up. To top it off, the front door knocker sounded. I shuffled out to see who was there. It was Andrew Giles, in a beautifully cut grey wool suit, white shirt, and blue silk tie. I barely recognised him. He looked smart, businesslike, and traditional. Nothing like the PR execs I was used to, in cool trainers and trendy casuals.

'I was wondering….' He stopped seeing I was close to tears. I had to say something.

'My marrow exploded,' I gasped.

'I beg your pardon?' he asked. 'Did you say marrow? Exploded?'

My shoulders sagged. 'Aunt Jen will be furious. I've wrecked her pantry.'

He shook his head with disbelief and came in. The man must think I'm an idiot, first I'd insisted his dog had to be called Hamburger, now this, I thought.

'It can't be that bad.' On reaching the pantry doorway, he stopped short. 'Oh… wow, it is rather a mess,'

I sniffed. 'Maybe I'll shut the door on it until tomorrow.'

'Hmm, I wouldn't. If it dries, you might never get it clean. I don't know whether marrow stains. It doesn't smell of vegetable though? It's more like booze?'

'It is, well was, marrow rum. I thought I'd try to make some.'

His shoulders shook with suppressed laughter. I managed a weak grin. If the room wasn't in such a state, it would be funny.

'There's a bucket in the corner. Let's make a start cleaning up. Where's the detergent? Flash floor cleaner? It'll have to be powerful.'

'You don't need to do that. Besides…' I'd noticed as I followed him to the pantry that he looked pretty sexy in the well cut suit. 'You're not dressed to scrub a floor.'

'I had a client presentation earlier, only flew back from Finland four hours ago. There are overalls in the car for site visits. I'll grab them and change.'

'Really? You don't have to.' My voice sounded unconvincing. I didn't know how to tackle the mess, especially after my wine.

'What are neighbours for? Show me where to change.' As he removed his jacket, I smelt a faint trace of musky aftershave.

He must have left the front door open, because two minutes later Hamburger appeared and scoffed lumps of fermenting vegetable flesh. I'd have let him; less to clear up, but Andrew grabbed his collar.

'Oh, no you don't, Jet. The last thing I need is a drunk or poisoned sheepdog. I've promised to move the flock to the top field for Dad this weekend.'

Hamburger didn't look pleased. Whether that was because of the name or being stopped from eating the marrow, I wasn't certain.

I found a scrubbing brush and scoured the floor tiles in the furthest corner as Drew began with the worst part; the gunge that covered the shelf around the marrow. Methodically, he cleared tins and jars out into the kitchen, then wiped and cleaned the shelves and wall. I changed his water, washed the jars, then got back to the floor. Space was tight in the pantry. Once I was out of my corner, we kept bumping into each other, then apologising.

I chatted about all the things I was doing in the village while he listened. It was companionable, working together, and the room looked much better. He spotted lumps of marrow on the ceiling and fetched the steps from the shed to wipe it clean. I'd never have reached; thank goodness he was here.

After an hour's grafting, I stopped and grinned at him. 'The pantry looks pretty good. It smells of booze, but not in an unpleasant way, more unusual. Hopefully, it will evaporate before Jen returns.'

'It was a shambles. You've got marrow in your hair. Come here and I'll wipe it off.'

I closed my eyes as he dabbed at my parting. He hesitated. A silence followed, so I asked, 'Is there more? Don't worry, it'll wash out in the morning.'

He coughed, tweaked my nose gently, then said, 'It's gone now. We ahh, make a good cleaning team. We could set up in business; *Mop and Bucket*.'

'Mmm, can't say cleaning is my thing, and it doesn't pay well. I suspect meetings in Finland mean you could earn more. I'm only relieved it hasn't stained the walls and ceiling. Oh, why did you call? Surely you didn't hear the explosion in the car? '

His face coloured. 'No, I got back earlier than expected. I thought might take you up on that offer of a drink. Introduce myself properly.'

'You deserve some wine. There are two glasses left in the bottle.'

He looked at his watch. 'I texted Dad I'd be home by nine. He'll have my supper waiting. I should get on.'

I nodded, uncertain whether I was relieved or disappointed.

'Thanks anyway. I'll owe you the wine.'

Drew

38

It had been hard not laughing out loud when I'd arrived at our neighbours, but the woman was practically in tears, so I bit my lip and kept it in. An exploding marrow, seriously? When I saw the mess in her aunt's pantry, I understood why she was upset.

Cleaning a pantry, after a three-hour drive from the airport wasn't in my plans, but what could I have done but offer to help? The tiny room smelt like a brewery.

As Amy scrubbed the floor next to me, I felt my body respond; had to avert my eyes from her bottom as she wiped and rinsed. She chatted on about walks and Zumba whilst I tried and failed to concentrate on what she was saying. Unable to reply with more than yes or no, I was mesmerised by the fine golden hairs on her neck and arms which glimmered in the overhead electric light's glow every time she reached to wipe the wall. I had to look away and was relieved the overalls hid my interest. I undid my shirt collar as sweat trickled down my neck. God, I must be desperate. Might GP Tracy be the solution? She was intelligent, attractive and divorced, the same as me. I'd text her later, see if she was up for a second date.

After we'd finished, Amy thanked me, but I spotted a lump of marrow in her hair and offered to remove it. She closed her eyes as I picked it off. Her lips were so soft and absurdly kissable, I didn't know what to do with myself. The urge to crush them with my own took me aback, silenced me. I coughed, then tweaked her nose as if she was three, then made an excuse when she offered me a glass of wine. Wanted to get away. What on earth was this woman doing to me?

I got back and told Dad why I was late and about the marrow. He'd laughed for the first time in ages.

'What's she like?' he asked.

'Pretty, mid-thirties, bit ditsy. Jet seems to like her.'

Sharp eyes gazed at me. 'Sounds a cutie. Why did you stop there on your way home?'

'She offered me a drink when we met last. I was being neighbourly, taking up her suggestion.'

'Neighbourly, I see.'

'It has been a long week, OK. And, and to be honest, the first time I saw her, I shouted. I've been feeling guilty. I was rude. She's all right, but not my type, if you're wondering. I prefer dark-haired women like, like, well, you know who. Once bitten. The project in Finland is taking all my energy; last thing I want or need is a woman in my life.'

I reflected, she isn't the sort I'm attracted to. I go for slim elegant brunettes, intellectual equals; not curvy, argumentative blondes.

Chapter 6

Amy

Back to volunteer in the shop on Monday, Linda and Gwen were in hysterics as I told them about the exploding marrow. I didn't mention Andrew helping. I knew better than upset Gwen again.

'I'm sorry I mentioned marrow rum now,' said Linda. 'I guess it would have tasted terrible.'

'It smelt pretty good. I was looking forward to it at Christmas. The video said it takes three months to brew.'

Gwen asked, 'Um, Amy, you put an airlock in the marrow?'

'Airlock? What's that?'

'When you make any wine, in a bottle or demijohn, the fermentation process produces carbon dioxide. It has to escape through a water airlock or else the pressure builds up and...'

I raised my eyebrows. 'Mmm, now you mention it, I saw some sort of twisty thing on YouTube. I made a hole with a knitting needle and hoped for the best. I should have sent for one.'

'Never mind, I've loads of bottles of elderflower wine to spare. That reminds me, I'm having a few people round for supper on Friday night. Nothing special and everyone will be older, but you look as if you could do with a decent meal.' Gwen winked at Linda as she spoke. 'Would you like to come? I'll give you a bottle then.'

'That would be lovely. You know I am a vegetarian?'
I said and pushed away a fleeting thought that if
Andrew Giles was passing, he still wouldn't get his
wine. I suspected he'd had more than enough of me
after the clear up operation last week. He'd go straight
home. What an odd man, living with his father at
weekends, despite what sounded like a decent job.
Didn't he have a place of his own?

Over the next few days, two bottles of homemade
wine appeared on my doorstep as news of the marrow
went around the village. I was mortified but had to
laugh; people were making me welcome.

I got to Gwen's at seven on Friday and she
welcomed me with a hug.

'Amy, lovely to see you. What a pretty dress.
Prosecco?'

She wore an elegant silk kimono jacket
embroidered with mauve dragons and wide black
trousers. The purple picked up a silver tint to her hair
that was new. Everything about Gwen was neat, tidy,
and controlled.

'Thanks, and that hair colour suits you,' I said.

An aroma of five spice and soy sauce filled the
house; whatever was she cooking? Four guests
waited in a low beamed long lounge, furnished with
oriental tables, vases and thick silky rugs set on a
gleaming parquet floor. An enormous log fire burnt in
the grate, its glow reflecting in the tiny straw bubbles
of our Prosecco.

After half an hour, she led us into her dining room.
Six tall candles flickered on the table, their reflections

glinting off crystal glasses, a decanter of red wine and a cut-glass bowl of late pink roses.

'How beautiful,' I said.

'Yes, it's how my parents liked it. I never changed this room; had no cause to when I came back.'

'Came back?'

'I nursed out in Hong Kong for thirty years.' She bustled away to fetch the first course.

'Does Gwen live alone?' I asked the man to my right, Charles.

'Yes, she never married, although it is hard to believe she didn't have plenty of offers. Gwen was a looker when she was younger,' he said. His wife shot him a look of irritation.

'I can imagine her in a starched uniform ensuring the hospital ran efficiently at all times.'

'So can I,' Charles agreed with a leer and sipped at his glass. A sharp elbow to the ribs from his wife came close to his spilling the wine as I rolled my eyes at the other guests.

Gwen presented me with a subtle spiced aubergine stew, with venison for everyone else, served on fine bone china. She'd flavoured the classic dishes with an Asian twist.

Gwen made me recount the marrow story again. As I concluded, I said, lifting my eyes heavenward, 'It's all I'm going to be remembered for in Talwern. Would you believe two people have left bottles of wine on my doorstep? One of rhubarb and one of elderflower.'

Gwen laughed. 'Not me gossiping, I promise, but Linda does like to share a funny story. At the end of the evening, Gwen said, 'I'll get you your coat, along

43

with a bottle of my elderflower, you can tell me which you like best.'

'Don't think about giving an opinion,' warned Charles. 'It's risky enough being a judge in the village show and entries there are anonymous.'

I walked back to the cottage, cheered by the excellent food and drink. When I arrived, yet another bottle waited on the step. Not more dodgy home-brew, I thought. It wasn't; it was a bottle of Pinot Grigio. Andrew had called by.

Drew

The weekend started badly. My flight from Belfast to Bristol delayed by three hours, yet again I didn't get home until after nine. I had warned Dad not to wait, and picked up a bottle of wine at the airport. All week long I'd looked forward to dropping by to see my new neighbour; find out what scrapes she'd got into since I saw her last. When I drove past, I was disappointed to find the cottage in darkness. Presumably she had better things to do on Friday nights than spend them driving back from London. I left the bottle on the doorstep anyway.

Dad's mood hadn't improved. Morose and monosyllabic, he had little to say when I got home. I recognised the cocoa cup I'd used on Sunday evening unwashed in the sink, along with three dishes.

'Dad, what have you eaten this week? The loaf in the bread bin is mouldy.'

'Couple of ready meals from the freezer.'

'I can't see the plates in the washing-up bowl?'

44

'Ate them from the plastic dish. What's the point of dirtying china?'

'For goodness' sake, what's got into you? You haven't changed your clothes all week, have you?'

He shrugged.

'You need to cheer up, do something for pleasure. Tell you what, let's go out tomorrow. I'll book the Walnut Bush. It's your favourite. You shower and get dressed up, I will too. We'll celebrate your birthday early.'

'Whatever you say. There is not much to enjoy about growing older. You wait.'

Chapter 7

Amy

Next morning, the knocker sounded. A short, red-faced man in dirty jeans and a worn checked shirt stood outside. An ancient red tractor, engine running with smoke pouring from a chimney set in its bonnet, chugged outside the gate.

'Sorry to wake you early on a Saturday, but I usually cut Jen's hedge for her when I'm doing my fields,' he said. 'I know she's away, but the cutting arm is on. It'll only take fifteen minutes. I top it and cut the outside. Jen trims inside the garden.'

'Thanks, of course, that'd be fab. How much will I owe you?'

'Jen gives me a jar of blackcurrant jam and a couple of quid for a pint in the Boar.'

'Great, there's plenty of jam in the pantry. I'll have it ready when you're done.'

'I usually get a cup of tea and biscuit too. It's a fair way back to my farm.'

The tractor roared into action. The cutting arm flailed, mincing the hedge in moments, twigs and branches flew everywhere. Inside, I put on the kettle, found his jam, wiped off a splodge of marrow gunk and took it outside, along with two mugs of tea and a fiver. The farmer sat legs crossed on Jen's garden bench waiting, while the tractor's engine spluttered in the background.

'Can't stop it, it may not start up again,' he nodded at the old machine. 'Been hearing about you, miss. Commute to Bristol?'

'Yes, I'm in PR, working with the food industry, help them sell more. I mostly work online, in social media.'

'Not a proper job then; never mind you'll find something better in time, or find a fella to marry you.'

My mouth dropped open.

'Heard about the busting marrow too. You'll learn. Next year's batch will be all right I 'spect. I'm told Andrew Giles helped you clear up. Here till nine at night?'

'He was passing and offered. How did you know, hear I mean?' I asked, bemused.

'Can't park a fancy car like that on the road and not get noticed. Nice boy, Andrew. Had it tough though.'

Intrigued, insulted and amused, I had to ask, 'How has he had it tough?'

'Well, then.' The man looked around as if someone might overhear us, as if there were crowds waiting in Jen's blackcurrant bushes to listen to him gossip. 'His mother left when he was a slip of a lad, five or six. Took him with her to the city. Cardiff, I ask you. Only let him come home every other weekend to visit his dad. How's a boy to learn to farm in two days a fortnight? The Gileses had over a hundred acres and a big herd. Raymond's had to scale back now, of course.' He left a dramatic pause.

Impossible not to ask. 'Why has Mr Giles scaled back?'

'Because he's poorly. Stroke three years ago. Forced to rent out most of his acres. Kept the sheep,

47

but both the beef and dairy herd had to go; Raymond couldn't manage milking twice a day. He's not finding it easy although Andrew comes home to help every weekend he can.'

He took a deep swig of his tea.

'Andrew doesn't live with his father then?'

'Got his own place, out somewhere near Abergavenny.'

I couldn't resist. 'His wife stays there while Andrew visits, I expect?'

He looked at me knowingly and tapped the side of his nose. 'Like father, like son. Andrew is divorced. That family always had trouble with women.'

He lurched to his feet and made for his tractor. 'Mind out for exploding marrows, young lady,' he said, and clambered up to drive off.

I sat back on the bench with my tea and mulled over the last ten minutes. What a relic from another age; how dare he suggest mine wasn't a real job. The cheek of the man. Still interesting to learn more about my neighbours in Rooks Row. Drew was single. I wondered what he did in the week.

At seven thirty, that evening the phone rang. It was Verity, asking if I'd like to pop round for an hour. Something in her voice told me she was upset. I agreed and glanced at the wine rack. I picked up the Pinot, but hesitated. Andrew Giles might drop by one evening. We'd try the rhubarb wine instead.

I set off for Verity's. A hundred yards from her gate, a familiar sage green Range Rover pulled up. Andrew was at the wheel, his father beside him. I noticed

Andrew's eyes flick to the bottle; and was relieved I hadn't taken his gift. I smiled politely at the man in the passenger seat. He didn't look unduly frail, a sixty odd year old, weather-beaten face with piercing brown eyes and a mop of dark hair, an older version of his son.

He nodded in return.

Andrew said, 'It's Dad's birthday in a couple of weeks; he's sixty. We're off to The Walnut Bush outside Abergavenny to celebrate.'

'Happy Birthday, Mr Giles. You're looking smart. It must be a fancy restaurant?'

Drew replied for them both. 'It is; luckily I left my suit in the wardrobe last week, after our,' he coughed, 'clean up operation.'

His father grinned. Yet another person who'd heard about the marrow incident. He looked at the bottle in my hand, then said, 'Rhubarb wine, a home brew. Be careful, it'll be powerful.'

'Verity and I will try not to overdo it.' I told him.

Of course we did. Verity's eyes were red and puffy as she stood in the doorway.

She led me into the kitchen, turned and said, 'Ben gone out again. Off to a Box of Frogs gig in Talybont. It was our anniversary in the week. Ben hadn't forgotten, but as it was a few days ago and we couldn't find a babysitter, he told me we'd go somewhere next weekend instead. Said he'd promised Simon he would watch the band if he could.'

'Bastard,' I sympathised, 'but next time call me. I could have baby sat.' I wasn't so much annoyed for

Verity, as affronted for myself. Why had Simon asked Ben to the gig and not me?

Verity took my bottle, directed the corkscrew into it with venom, and pulled the cork. 'The kids are asleep. Let's get smashed.'

To my surprise, the wine was delicious, sweet and way too easy to drink. As it took effect, we shared complaints. I told her all about Alan, and how he was handsome and super cool, but easily bored. He kept changing his job and the last change he met another woman.

'To make it worse, she's older and not particularly pretty, divorced with a six-year-old.' My eyes teared up. 'And now she's got Alan. I hate her.'

Verity poured herself a second enormous glass of wine, then complained about Ben. 'It was great living here at first. We both enjoyed the lifestyle; walks, gardening, DIY. He's so busy that he often has to stay three nights in London. His mother spoils him; does his washing and ironing; there's a meal ready when he gets in. She doesn't make him do chores, says that's for her and his dad.

'When he comes back, he expects to be waited on. Initially, he loved trimming the box hedges, pruning and mowing. Now he says as I'm home all week I should do it in my spare time. I've two children to look after. What spare time?'

'Absolutely right.'

We'd made quick work of the rhubarb wine; the bottle soon emptied.

'There's rum in the cupboard. Let's make mojitos,' Verity giggled. 'All men are the same, selfish to the core.'

I told her about the creeps I'd dated in the past; how they appeared charming at first, but one way or another turned out to be heels.

As the list continued, Verity nodded and said, 'They sound like a cross between Ben as he is now and Simon. At least Ben is not a womaniser. I trust him, but honestly, Amy, Simon's cast a spell on him. It's a bromance. Not, not in a sexual way, more Ben comes home exhausted on a Friday night, falls asleep in the chair, then, if he wakes early enough, he'll wonder whether Simon's about. He's always dropping his name into conversation. He should ask about the kids, or me, not some bloke from the pub.'

'Sounds like a second adolescence.'

'Exactly.'

We jumped as the kitchen door opened half an hour later.

It was Ben. 'Hi, nice to see you Amy.' He attempted to give Verity a hug. Ignoring her stiff posture, he said, 'Looks like you girls have been having fun? There's an empty bottle and the rum and lemonade are out. We haven't had cocktails in ages, have we doll?'

Verity glared at him. In an ominously low voice she said, 'No, not had much chance, have I?'

They were gearing up for a row. I made my excuses and left, relieved to be out of there.

On the way home, I had to laugh. I'd drunk too much and walking in a straight line was impossible. As I wove back and fore looking up at the stars, my heart felt lighter; a trouble shared, they say. It had been nice to have someone to confide in. Lucky I hadn't driven. The rhubarb wine packed a punch, but it was delicious.

At Well Cottage, I fumbled in my pocket for my keys and tried to open the front door. The lock had been stiff for a week or so, and tonight it was worse than ever. I took the key out and forced it back in, then turned it firmly. It snapped. The top half held in my fingers, the rest jammed cleanly in the keyhole. It wouldn't budge when I attempted to extract it.

Oh no, I was locked out. What should I do? I could have returned to Verity's but remembering the atmosphere there, decided against. I glanced up. The narrow rectangular upper window of the bathroom was ajar. I'd get in that way.

My aunt's ladder hung on brackets on the shed wall; aluminium is light, should be able to manage that, I thought. I lifted it. Mmm, heavier than expected, but I slowly dragged it along the path. It was tricky to lift, but I finally levered it into position.

I put a tentative foot on the first rung, but stopped when headlights from the road illuminated the front of the house. A car braked to a halt. My heart sank; of course it was Andrew and his father, on their way home from Abergavenny.

Seconds later, Andrew shouted from outside, 'What are you doing? Why is there a ladder up there?' He pushed at the gate, expression incredulous, and walked toward me. Mr Giles limped behind him. Both looked at me expectantly.

'I, um, my key, it got schtuck, I mean stuck. It broke.' I held the fractured key towards them. I snorted, trying not to laugh at the look on their faces; horror on Andrew's, perplexity on his father's.

Andrew's voice was accusing. 'You're tipsy, aren't you?'

'A little.' I tittered helplessly. Everything seemed funny. 'That rhubarb wine was as strong as you warned, Mr Giles.'

'So it seemed a good idea to climb a ladder in the dark?' Andrew asked.

'I can't stay outside in the cold all night. It's a plan. I'll be up in seconds. You can hold the ladder, if you like.' I turned and climbed the first three rungs.

A firm hand pulled me down.

'No, you won't. Even if you don't fall off in the state you're in, how will you clamber through that gap?'

'Ish fine, no problem at all. The bathsss under the window. I'll put one leg…' I stopped. Actually, stretching from the ladder and levering myself through the small upper window might be tricky. Could I reach?

Father and son exchanged glances. Andrew removed his jacket and held it out to his father.

'I'll go up. At least I'm sober.'

Mr Giles said, 'I know how much you paid for that suit. Bespoke, from Jermyn Street for your sister's wedding. You're not climbing up in those trousers, Drew. Not to help a daft…' He fell silent. I wondered what word he'd been about to use.

'We can't leave her outside all night or watch her break her neck, can we? It's easier if I do it.'

His father's jaw set and he crossed his arms. 'No, you'll ruin your trousers. Take them off. Go up in your trunks.'

Andrew looked from one of us to the other. 'For God's sake, you're as bad as each other.'

He removed the elegant grey trousers to reveal pale blue trunks. I giggled again as his father suppressed a smile.

Andrew glared at us, checked the ladder footing and carefully climbed up. As I'd guessed, reaching the open window wasn't easy. He leant precariously and stretched a over to the window frame. As he pivoted onto the frame, the ladder wobbled, but his father's foot was firm on the bottom rung. He swung himself up and went through head first. There was a thump and 'sodding hell' as Drew tumbled into the bath.

His father winced. 'You OK?' he called.

A minute later, Andrew appeared at the front door. Still glaring, he held it wide open for me. Wordlessly, he took his trousers and dressed.

'Um, thank you,' I said. 'I'm very grateful. I'll be off to bed.'

Next morning my head pounded, waves of nausea washed over me every few minutes. It wasn't only the hangover. Had I attempted to climb a ladder after half a bottle of rhubarb wine and two mojitos last night? How mortifying. Whatever must Drew think of me? I'd a glass in my hand practically every time we'd met. He must think I'm a lush. Thank goodness he stopped me from trying to clamber up to the window. In return I had laughed helplessly at him when he'd been kind.

I cringed, recollecting the thud as Drew landed in the bath, then remembered his muscular thighs climbing the ladder. Not bad, I mused, under that elegant, traditional suit, not so bad. A second thought struck; I groaned. Aunt Jen kept a spare back door key under the big lavender flower pot. I could have used that to get in. My stomach lurched and I rushed to the loo to vomit.

Drew

The end of our evening out entertained Dad. He had picked at a delicious meal in the restaurant and refused a dessert, said he'd no appetite. After I climbed the ladder, he'd chuckled to himself all down the lane to the farm. It was the first time I'd heard him laugh since I told him about the exploding marrow. What a clown that woman was.

'Eh, you looked a right idiot in your underpants, socks and shoes on that ladder. Me and that niece of Jen's had a real giggle,' he said.

'Thanks, it was because of you I was in my underwear.'

'No point in spoiling a perfectly nice suit, well not unless you wanted to impress the girl. May not have done that.'

'OK, OK. Don't rub it in, I looked ridiculous. Why would I care if I impressed her? Told you, she's not my type.'

Dad couldn't stop himself. 'She was tiddly wasn't she? I'm glad we stopped. Wouldn't like to find her in a heap with a broken neck tomorrow. I blame that rhubarb wine. Bet it was Selwyn's. He adds sugar to the bottles after the first fermentation; it strengthens the brew.'

My stomach lurched with embarrassment. What must I have looked like? A row with Dad over climbing up wouldn't have impressed, either. I'd no choice but to give in. How could that woman be so silly as to think of climbing a ladder drunk?

Chapter 8

Amy

Finally three weeks had passed and I was excited to meet Simon again. A guitarist in a band; OK, a small local band, but he was good looking and confident. The sort of bloke a schoolgirl dreams of. Maybe this time? I remembered my resolution to take a break from men while I was in Talwern. I'd blown that idea. Stop running away with yourself, I thought. You always do this; play it cool for once.

I worked the rock chick look for the night and dug out my blue suede Levi's. I hadn't worn them for years, so they were tight, arguably too tight, but surely that's what rock chicks wore? Heels, a tee with diamante encrusted white and pink Vegas sign and my denim jacket completed the outfit. I back combed my hair, using loads of hairspray for height and volume, then applied shimmering eyeshadow and lipstick; very 80s. I missed my nights out in Bristol. Alan and I loved clubbing when we first met. After he started 'working late,' I partied with the girls and dressed up, anyway.

I drove the half mile to the pub because of the heels. It'd mean I wouldn't have to rely on Simon for a lift; rather early to invite him back.

He sat on a stool in the bar of the Black Boar, and whistled when I arrived. 'You look great,' he said, 'really cool. Love the jeans; I've a leather pair for when I'm on stage. What can I get you? Cider?'

I'd fancied a gin and tonic, but agreed to the cider as suggested, and stood beside him in the full room.

Simon chatted enthusiastically; told me all about his work.

'I manage a music shop in Hereford. You'd be amazed at the stars who drop by; Ellie Goulding, Robert Plant; I know them all and they give me free tickets to shows.'

While he talked about the Powys and Herefordshire music scene, I looked around. My feet pinched as I stood beside his stool.

I was the only woman in the bar not wearing flats, but as I flirted, I didn't care. An hour later, Ben pushed open the door and made a beeline for us.

'Verity's not with you?'

'Nah, wasn't sure I'd get back in time from London. Not worth getting a babysitter for half an hour in the pub,' he replied. 'Drink, Amy?'

He bought me a second half of cider, along with two pints of Butty Bach for Simon and himself. Then started a discussion on plagiarism in recent song releases. I tried to join in their conversation, but it got more and more heated. I glanced around the bar, a mixed crowd, but I recognised one or two faces. When a stool freed up, I fetched it and jumped as an old man pinched my bum. Surely no one did that anymore?

It was closing time before either of them paid me any attention. Ben had the audacity to ask for a lift home.

Simon grinned. 'You're probably safer with her than on my Norton,' he said.

A motor bike! Thank goodness I hadn't walked. He'd downed at least three pints, but as his blue eyes gazed winningly at me, my irritation washed away. He was so handsome, and as a musician, he was bound to love music.

'Be careful on the way home,' I told him.

He kissed my hand. 'We'll meet again soon.' He hadn't asked for my number.

Ben steered me out of the pub, tumbled into my passenger seat, and belched.

'Oops, sorry.' He'd caught up with Simon's drinking in the hour before closing. 'Glad you and Verity have hit it off,' he said. 'She is lonely here because I'm away at least two or three nights a week. Hey, we four should go for a Nepalese at the weekend. There's a great curry house up the road.'

Yes, and I'm sure you going out on Saturday night and rolling back pissed helps Vee's loneliness, I thought to myself, smiled, then said, 'That'd be great.' After all, Simon didn't have my number.

On Sunday, I woke to another glorious autumn day. No excuse not to run before breakfast, so I threw on my lycra and a grey sweatshirt. After a warm up, I set off up the mountainside; best to get the hardest stretch out of the way first. Gold and amber leaves crunched under my trainers as I ran through oak and beech woods, then climbed up onto a path through bronzed bracken, high above the lake and village. Looking down, I saw the nearest field was full of sheep, bleating and running in every direction, and glimpsed Hamburger chasing after them.

I stopped to watch. He seemed to charge one way, then the other. It didn't look right. A figure in blue overalls stood at the gate at the bottom of the field, Andrew.

He whistled frantically, ordering "Jet" right and left again and again. His shouts confused me. How a dog could understand them, I'd no idea. I jogged on down the path towards the them. As I arrived, Hamburger ran up, jumped the gate, then walked in repeated figures of eight against my legs, anxious and unhappy. I bent to stroke and reassure him.

Andrew said, 'Damn dog, no use at all. We were told his training wasn't complete, but I'd say it's hardly started. Only good to keep women company and eat biscuits. He's useless.'

I bridled, and fancied Hamburger did as well.

'It's how you treat him that's the problem,' I said, ice in my tone. I thought about how men round here seemed to insult women all the time. The sheep had settled and grouped in the far corner by the hedge. I opened the gate a fraction, fondled Hammy's ear, and whispered quietly into it, 'Fetch, fetch the sheep, good boy.'

Hamburger shot off, but aimed for the further side of the field this time. He slunk low and ran toward the corner where the sheep gathered. They moved towards us when Hamburger chivvied them along, with low growls. As the animals got nearer, one darted to the left.

'Away, Hammy,' I called. He did and peeled smoothly anticlockwise to herd the lone sheep back into the crowd.

'Open the gate if you want them to come through,' I told Drew. 'We should stand back, not to spook them.'

Andrew's face was a mixture of disbelief and disgust. I'd proven him entirely wrong. This time I was the one able to snigger. I knew the dog had done all the work himself, my calls had been irrelevant, but Drew didn't.

'I'll get on with my run,' I said, trying not to gloat. Then I shouted over my shoulder, 'Thanks again for the help with the marrow. That glass of wine's still on offer.'

Drew

Sally and I met to discuss a tricky HR problem in the week.

Afterwards she asked, 'How are you and Tracy getting on? Have you set up another date?'

'We're fine, have texted a few times, but no, not yet.'

'Why not? It's been three weeks since you saw her. Try to appear interested, Drew, for goodness' sake.'

'OK, OK. I'll see when she's free.'

'Honestly, you're hopeless.' She raised her eyebrows in mock despair.

Angel buzzed to say Daniel Kelly was waiting to discuss the Helsinki project and Sally left.

'Send him in.' I grinned to myself. Two could play at cupid; I'd try matchmaking myself. The boy always hurried to the coffee maker whenever Angel fetched me my morning flat white. The entire office watched as he'd try to charm her. Angel appeared impervious, but once I'd spotted her turn back when Daniel was on the telephone. She's wait until he'd put down the receiver, and then fetched my coffee. I suspected she liked him, but didn't know how to show that.

'Take a note of the meeting, will you, Angel?' I asked as he came through the door. Panic flashed over her face. I usually took my own notes and got her to type them up. She was a great PA, but shorthand wasn't one of her strengths.

Daniel and I discussed how to address the early challenges of the project; the environmental survey had thrown up the usual rare insect and amphibian suspects.

'At least we didn't find Viking longship burials when the bloody archeologists came in,' I joked. Archeologists had seriously delayed two of our current projects after excavating pottery and tile on the sites.

Ridiculous, one find was Tudor. So what if there might have been a hunting lodge built there in the past? All they needed to do was join the National Trust to visit intact Tudor buildings; Windsor and Hampton Court, for a start.

My blood pressure rose, remembering the arguments in an Essex village hall last month. The attendees, of course, were delighted to stop the development. They agreed with the archeological team, that extending the dig for another two months was vital to understand the site. In the mean time, the developers and my team had to twiddle their thumbs, and our clients lost money.

'That reminds me, I have to pop and check something with HR,' I told them. 'I'll be two ticks. Wait here, please.'

I left the pair in my office for fifteen minutes, knowing it would force them to talk for longer than the press of the coffee machine button. When I came back, the boy grinned, looking delighted with himself. Angel's expression was as inscrutable as ever.

After he left, I asked, 'Did Daniel ask you out then?'

'How did you guess?'

'Angel, he's been watching your every move in the office for months.'

I met Tracy for our second date on the next Friday night, near her home in Clapham. My palms sweated as I walked through the heavy rain between the tube station and the restaurant. Would she ask me back to hers? If she did, what would it mean? Oh God, do I have to go through this again? I thought.

Until Stephanie, I'd found dating difficult. Never knew what women expected. Stephanie directed me every step of the way. I didn't have to think after we met. She told me where we'd go and when. Taken me shopping for what she described as, signature designer jeans and roll necks, shortly after we'd started seeing each other.

I reached the restaurant, a cute local Italian. Tracy was prompt and sat waiting for me at a table, nibbling on the complimentary breadsticks. I ordered a bottle of Barolo and we shared a whitebait starter. I'd gone for the Bolognese; slurping spaghetti would break the ice. I talked about Dad and his stroke for a while. She offered wise words, but I picked up she didn't want to talk about medicine, so switched to the subject of my office matchmaking. Keep it light, I thought. After she told me about last week's arguments with her husband over alimony and pensions, I told her about Amy and her exploding marrow, which made her giggle.

'Drew, that's the first story you've said with any emotion. Amy sounds sweet. You let your guard down for once.'

I gazed at the red-checked tablecloth and shuffled my cutlery. 'I'm old-fashioned, was brought up not to show emotions. Never to let it show when I minded.'

'Mmm, but in the long term that doesn't work, does it? Stops you getting close to people, it is a barrier,' she said.

After a shared tiramisu, Tracy looked deep into my eyes and said, 'Drew, I like you a lot. It's been another great evening, but has proven I'm not ready. It's too soon for me. I'm not sure you're open to a genuine relationship right now, either.'

I could have argued. She might have listened, agreed to meet again, but actually it was a relief. I didn't fancy her. I liked her, enjoyed her company, but… there was no spark. My pulse didn't race when she looked up at me, not the way it had with Amy in that pantry.

I faked a histrionic groan, then said, 'Think how disappointed Sally will be.' We laughed again and agreed it would be nice to meet as friends; both of us knowing full well it would never happen.

I drove back to Talwern on Saturday afternoon. Dad was OK, but fussing that he hadn't moved the sheep, and that the grazing was too sparse on the lower field.

'OK, I'll take out the new dog and move them tomorrow morning, then take him for a walk.'

Sunday dawned crisp and bright as I left for the top fields with Jet. I was glad to be outside and in Breconshire, not cooped up in a boardroom. A lone jogger ran on the ridge above us. Looking across the hillsides to the mountains beyond, I felt wedded to the land. That my ancestors farmed these fields for generations made it even more precious. On days like this, I wondered whether moving away, forging a new direction, was a mistake. Dad and my grandfather, they'd been happy here. Should I have stayed? Maybe I'd have met someone, had a family to carry things on.

Jet enjoyed being in the open, did as he was told until we reached the sheep, when everything fell to bits. I led him into the field, took out my whistle and blew. Two shrill peeps carried over the field. Meg would have walked on and stood, but Jet stared at me, with no idea what to do.

My whistles became more urgent. The puppy ran in circles, scattering the sheep in every direction. I shouted 'Left, Jet, left.' Nothing happened, useless animal.

The runner stopped at the gate beside me, flushed from running, two stray curls fell from the pony tail holding her blond hair, and wearing an old red tee shirt and lycra leggings. No make up, bare faced, skin glowing, she looked delectable.

Breathless, Amy asked, 'Hi, having problems?'

It was my new neighbour and she would not be impressed by how irritated I'd sounded with the collie. The scent of her, deodorant fresh, mixed with a musk made me swallow. I had to say something fast and stupidly told her the dog was half trained.

Frowning, she had the gall to suggest it was my fault and implied that I was wrong. I've spent years herding sheep with Meg. Annoyed by her attitude I replied that Jet was only any good at eating biscuits. She glared at me, bent to calm Jet down, stroked his fur, then whispered softly to him.

To my amazement, she sent the dog into the field and gathered in the spooked flock down to us. How the hell did she manage that? As far as I knew, she had no farming background; word in the village was that she worked in IT.

The woman smirked as she ordered me to open the gate. I didn't know what to say. To cap my humiliation, she thanked me for helping her clean up the week before, then jogged away.

I couldn't tear my eyes from her retreating bottom as she disappeared down the road. Lycra is too damn revealing.

Chapter 9

Amy

After Monday's Zumba class Verity said, 'Ben and Simon have arranged for us to go for a curry on Saturday, if you're free? We've found a babysitter.'

'That'd be nice, but I thought Ben was taking you out for your anniversary this weekend?'

'So did I, but he said this would be more fun. It probably will too. At least we won't spend the evening bickering.

'There's something I need to tell you. Ben came back early from the pub last Sunday because Simon was off to see his latest girlfriend. Said she'd been giving him grief for going out all the time, and that he was fed up with her.'

'Sooo, he's not single then?' I asked.

'No, supposed to have a string of girlfriends. Simon told him you were cool, though. He's likely lining you up to be next.'

I smiled with satisfaction, but noticed that Verity's expression showed misgivings.

'You sure, Amy? You don't need to be let down again.'

As I walked home, I pondered what she'd said. Could she be right? Simon was my usual type. Why should I let his having a girlfriend put me off? All's fair in love and war, after all. I felt uncomfortable wondering whether it was what Alan's divorcee had concluded, when stole him from me?

We met Simon in the Boar on Saturday evening after Ben and Verity picked me up on the way. Ben said Verity would drive us home. The pub was cosy and packed with locals. Selwyn, who'd cut Jen's hedge, sat beside a grey permed woman I recognised from Zumba, one of the baggy tracksuit bottom gang.

He called me over. 'Meet my wife. She's heard all about you. Not out with another bloke? Like moths to the flame, eh? Andrew Giles is over there. He was staring daggers a moment ago.'

I hadn't noticed Andrew sitting in the corner with a group of men in tweed jackets. He fitted right in, looked the same as the rest. I gave a friendly smile when I caught his eye, but Selwyn was right; he blanked me.

I went back to Verity, and Simon casually threw his arm over my shoulder. I'd have been pleased if the thought of Andrew watching hadn't disturbed me. We left after one drink. It was raining, so Simon suggested he'd leave his bike in the pub car park. He sat in the back beside me, took my hand, and placed it on his crotch. 'Nippy outside,' he laughed. Shocked, I pulled it away, cheeks burning red with embarrassment.

The Nepalese curry house was in a village five miles away. They chatted about music all the way. 'I prefer an authentic sound,' Verity said. 'For example why play, "Key to the Highway" in A like Clapton, when Charlie Segar wrote and played it in E?'

'Because it is funkier in the key of A, that why. Big Bill Broonzy's interpretation is great but the Dominoes' album is the definitive version,' Simon replied.

Ben acted as peacemaker. 'I like both. It was played at Duane Allman's funeral you know? He loved playing that track with Clapton.'

Music is pleasant, good to dance to, but it's not a big deal for me. The others held strong views on everything they talked about. I was excluded from their conversation.

When we reached the restaurant car park, Simon took my arm, winked and said, 'Music is my passion Amy, the thing I love above everything else. The women in my life have to accept that.'

'My passion is history; what lies beneath,' I replied. He raised an eyebrow and shrugged, uninterested. That line intrigued most people. They'd ask why at the very least. Mind you, Alan had never been interested, either; hadn't cared I'd given up what I loved for him.

Ben went back out to check he'd switched off the car headlights, so I popped to the ladies' room. As I came out, I noticed Simon and Verity, faces intense; they were arguing. I returned to an uncomfortable silence.

Simon explained, 'I made the mistake of suggesting Robert Plant's music is as worthwhile as Dave Brubeck or Thelonuis Monk's, but Vee disagrees.' He raised an ironic eyebrow and laughed. Verity's face had reflected fury. It seemed odd that she should feel so strongly about a composer. Was that really what they'd been discussing?

Ben returned from the car park and launched into a long debate about the merits of rock versus classical music, judging from her comments it appeared that Verity cared deeply about music, too. Talk turned to politics, then travel; finally I could join the conversation.

Simon and Ben ordered more rounds of Asian beer, as poppadoms and a plate of chutney arrived. The spicy Gurka curry mains tasted authentic at a fraction of Bristol prices. We split the bill at Simon's suggestion. The question of where we'd leave him loomed large in my mind.

Verity looked at me, her expression a warning. She said, 'We'll drop you by the Boar, and your bike then, Simon?'

'I'd thought we might go to Amy's for a nightcap first? You could leave me there, I can, ahh, walk back.'

Did I want Simon stopping for a coffee? I'd a suspicion he'd be hard to get rid of.

I said, 'I've a headache starting. Too much Cobra, I expect. Best if we call it a night.'

He recovered quickly. 'How about one at yours then, Ben?'

'Yeah, cool, I've got some craft cans in.'

I didn't dare look at Verity; what an anniversary celebration.

Drew

The local NFU rep organised a meeting in the Boar on Saturday night. They'd agreed to outline the next Welsh Government Rural Grants Scheme and the opportunities it offered. Dad refused to go.

'Not another bloody Government scheme. The EU ones were bad enough. I can't be bothered to jump through hoops for them again. All those on-line forms, with those damn paper pushers from Cardiff checking up on you all the time,' he said.

'It's an evening out. You never know, there could be something in it for us. I've read there's a set-aside scheme with money for woodland creation and restoration. They'll pay for new hedges too. I've been meaning to extend the woods next to the Nant field; it's too damp to plant crops and the sheep get foot rot. To be paid to plant native trees would be a bonus; alder and birch, along with hazel to coppice. What do you think?'

'I don't care. You go. The land's yours in trust, anyway. I'll not see trees grow. I'll be six feet under by the time they reach shoulder height.'

'Dad, you're sixty. You've twenty or more years in you. What ever are you talking about?'

He screwed up his eyes. 'Hell, surely not? I can barely walk around the farm with my leg. I'm hoping for another stroke, a big one.'

'Dad, don't even think that. What a dreadful thing to say. I'll go to the meeting, but a trip to the Boar would do you good. I wish you'd come.'

In the kitchen cupboard by the sink, it didn't surprise me to find four unopened boxes of blood pressure and aspirin pills. We rowed again. Dad refused to promise to take them until I threatened to call the doctor. Somehow, I had to get him to see Dr Davies. He was so depressed. Would he bother with the antidepressants? He swallowed his medication when I stood over him at weekends, but during the week?

71

In the Boar, my farming neighbours were surly with the NFU rep. Their response to the grants on offer, not dissimilar to Dad's. Selwyn's view summed up the reality of the new schemes. 'If you own land, it might help, make up for losing the EU subsidy, but if you're a tenant or rent fields, how can you plant for the future? I need cash to put food on the table. What use are hedges and woodlands? They won't feed anyone, not me or the British public.' He stalked off to sit with his wife.

Out of the corner of my eye, I watched Amy come in. She looked lovely in tight jeans, cowboy boots and a hunting jacket, really cute, and joined the new couple from The Oaks, who, of course, were with Simon Evans. My stomach churned as he draped an arm over Amy's shoulders. I became annoyed with myself. Why should I care if she hooked up with that lech?

She waved. I ignored her; cross to notice my heart pound. Did she have any idea about how Evans was with women? His reputation? Did her neighbours come to that? It astonished me he and Ben were friends.

Later, I asked Selwyn to cut our hedges and do a spot of ditching.

'Thanks, I'll be glad to have some money coming in,' he said. 'The wife's working the tills in Morrisons, but it's minimum wage. What she gets barely pays for our heating oil and petrol to get her to work. Cost of living's crippling.'

He nodded in Amy's direction. 'Pretty girl that niece of Jen's, Well Cottage. Works in an office in Bristol,

social media or some such nonsense. Seen her out
with that lot before.'

Chapter 10

Amy

It was the first Thursday of October, the date of next rambling group meeting. September in Talwern had flashed past. I'd offered to car share with Gwen and Verity, but in the end Verity took her youngest to the dentist, so it was Gwen and me. I picked her up on the way and followed her directions. We drove across the River Usk and past two ancient pubs. Gwen directed me to turn sharp left, over a picturesque canal swing bridge, then up a valley alongside a reservoir. At the end we came to stone bridge where, Gwen told me, a path led up to waterfalls and pleasant bathing pools in summer.

My Honda struggled on and up the steepest hill I'd ever seen. I prayed we wouldn't meet another car coming the other way, certain I'd panic and stall if it did. Finally, we emerged onto the top of the Beacon's plateau.

'We're going up there, Craig y Fan Du,' Gwen pointed to a rounded mountain. 'It's a great walk, steep, but once you're up, you won't believe the views.'

The ramblers' group waited in the car park, and we set off walking poles at the ready. The first section of the climb was the hardest, up steep steps past a waterfall and red leafed mountain ash trees. Above the tree line, bracken covered the mountain. Frosts had transformed the hillsides from green to warm browns and golds. I didn't chat like the others, but kept my energy to breathe and gaze around. It was so lovely. Why hadn't I climbed the Beacons before? Aunt Jen invited me regularly, but I stayed in the city, first London, then Bristol.

At last we reached a flat ridge and walked in single file along an edge, with a fall hundreds of feet to our right.

Gwen caught up with me. Amazing isn't it?'

At the front of the line, Helen pointed, and everyone stopped. The word 'kestrel' passed between us. To my right, the bird, a warm cinnamon shadow, hung motionless over the void, then soared away over the mountainside, hunting.

At the head of the valley, Helen called a halt. 'We'll eat here before going to the crash site; it would be disrespectful to do so at the memorial.'

The Wellington Bomber site took me aback. It was such a beautiful spot and so sad. The spot marked by a tangle of aluminium wreckage, along with a stone column, it's base laid with half a dozen faded poppy wreaths. The plane so nearly made it over the mountain all those years before. It crashed feet from the summit.

Gwen read aloud a simple inscription from the monument, 'At 0030 hours on 6th July 1942, Wellington bomber R1465, with a Canadian crew of five on a training flight from their base in Warwickshire, crashed, killing all on board. It is thought they were lost and descended through thick cloud to try to establish their position.'

Everyone was subdued and thoughtful for the first half mile; Gwen more than most, and asked me to drop her at her house rather than go on to the Black Boar.

Gwen invited me in for a coffee and explained. 'It took me aback the memorial. Those poor young men killed so far from home, such a short distance from safety, heartbreaking. Reminded me of Mother's tales of Aunt Lillie. The tragedy of her life, one terrible loss after another, and then to die so young, only twenty-six.'

'You said her fiancé was in the RAF?'

He was, but he wasn't the only one who died. Lillie had an admirer before she met her fiancée. One her family didn't approve of, Harold Giles. He adored her.

'A Giles? Was he from Rooks Row Farm?'

'Yes, Harry was the current owner's great uncle.'

I noticed the formality of her expression. How she didn't say my neighbour's name.

'Mother told me Harry Giles was a quiet boy, shy even, and Lillie supposedly wasn't very interested. Her family disapproved of him anyway, but there weren't many boys her age in the village, so they kept company for a while. When the war began, she joined the WAAFs, the Women's Auxiliary Air Force. They posted her to Flowerdown in Hampshire, where she had a wonderful time, was taught to fly. They moved her into the Air Transport Auxiliary, she became an 'Attagirl,' and delivered planes for the RAF as a ferry pilot. I suppose that was when she met her fiancé. He asked her to pose for the painting in my hall. Imagine, an artist and RAF pilot defending Britain against Germany; it must have been so romantic.

'Back in Talwern Harry was distraught that she'd left and got engaged. He was exempt from serving. All farmers were, the country needed them to produce food. He took it into his head that if she saw him in uniform, she'd think again. At the recruiting office in Brecon, Harry stood in line and joined the RAF as well. The poor lad died on his first operation after completing flight training.'

'How terrible! How old was he?'

'Twenty-two, the same age as my great aunt. The Gileses blamed Lillie, however baffling that sounds. When her fiancé died, his father bought a round of drinks for everyone in the Boar. What was worse, after the war, when my great aunt was admitted to the sanatorium in Sully with TB, Harry's mother stopped my grandmother outside the post office. Told her it served Lillie right. She called her a trollop.'

'That's awful.'

'My family never spoke to the Gileses again. They forbade me to have anything to do with them; difficult in a small village, believe me.'

She shrugged. 'That memorial brought Great Aunt Lillie's story flooding back. Don't mention it to anyone. No point in raking over old coals.'

'I won't, but goodness, it is such a sad tale.'

Gwen's eyes misted as she nodded her agreement.

On Sunday, I decided to go jogging at ten. The leaves had turned colour and glowed in the weak autumn sun. As I emerged from Well Cottage,

Hamburger ran towards me. Limping after him, face despondent, came Mr Giles.

'Lovely day,' I called.

'Suppose so. Trying to take this lad for a walk; Drew's in London. The pup is too young to be stuck inside all day. Needs more exercise than I can manage.'

He gestured towards Hamburger.

'Would you let him come with me? I'm off for a run to the church and will go on to the lake, as long as it's dry enough underfoot. To be honest, I'd like a dog with me. I feel exposed as a woman running alone and would be more comfortable if Hamburger came.'

Mr Giles nodded, 'I can see you might. I'd like you to have him with you, in fact. Good to be safe.'

'I could take him every day, except for Friday and Tuesday; that's when I work in Bristol. A routine would be good and force me not to put off running.'

'You'll be doing me a favour. Collies get unruly if they aren't exercised,'he said with a brief smile. It made him appear years younger.

Over the following days Hamburger and I enjoyed our runs. Hammy must have covered three times my distance, exploring scents and tearing up and down paths, tail wagging furiously. We developed a routine. On dry days, the farmer and Hamburger waited by the gate at the end of the lane at one pm. After a brief chat, usually about the weather, Hammy and I would set off. I left a tired dog back to the farmhouse an hour or so later. Mr Giles asked me to his sitting room for tea every few days. I knew people rarely called, so would stop for a chat, along with a cuppa and biscuit.

Three weeks later was Halloween. Verity was on the village school's Parents Teachers Association and had organised a scarecrow trail for the children. She'd offered to throw a fancy dress party after the judging on the Saturday night.

'It gets me out of doing anything for Guy Fawkes night. Wilf hates fireworks; cowers in the corner, whining. We'll pop to the Rotary Club display in Talybont instead. Would you mind helping?'

'I'd love to. What's the plan?'

'The kids will do the rounds, trick or treating and collecting sweets with the adults. Then everyone from the PTA comes back here for a party; a bonfire with barbecued sausages and onions, pumpkin soup, apple bobbing, hot chestnuts, big bowl of punch. All the usual.'

'I haven't bobbed for apples since I was seven. It's impossible, isn't it?'

She laughed. 'The men get competitive and manage it sometimes. I hate getting my face wet.'

'What will you wear?' she asked, 'I have a glamorous witch outfit from last year, I'll use.'

'I'll have to think. Who else is invited?'

She looked at me over reading glasses. 'Ben's invited Simon, if that's what you mean.'

I blushed and changed the subject.

That evening I searched for Halloween costumes on Amazon. I clicked buy on a hooded cape top that opened to wings with pointed ears on the hood, along with a pair of cobweb tights. I'd team it with my shortest black skirt, boots, and paint my nails red.

Next Saturday, I arrived at six. 'Wow, you look great,' Verity said. 'Pour yourself some punch. Could you butter the bread rolls for the sausages?' She took a long sip from the large glass beside her at the sink.

Vee had changed her mind about the glamorous witch and painted two of her teeth with dark brown nail varnish instead, then stuck a hideous luminous green lump on her chin.

'Um, well, you're, ahh, hideous.'

'Aren't I? The children screamed when they saw me. I may take the wart off later, but it's fun for now.' She poured herself another punch.

'Let's light the bonfire, ready for everyone to come back. Ben's put firelighters inside straw bundles in the middle.' She lit a spill, leant forward, and almost toppled headfirst into the heap of logs and branches.

'Let me do that,' I rushed out, and wondered how much she'd drunk before I'd arrived.

People trickled in to the garden with shrieks of laughter as everyone compared costumes. Ben returned to take charge of the barbecue, and soon the scent of frying sausages and smoke drifted over their garden. He tried to kiss Verity's cheek, but she turned away. I noticed him glance warily at her tumbler full of punch.

Simon arrived about nine, dressed as Jimmy Savile in a pale blue tracksuit, along with a gold medallion, sunglasses and cigar. He joined Ben and took control of the speaker system. I raised an eyebrow when he came over to talk.

'Jimmy was a monster, right?' he explained. 'It's Halloween. You make a cute vampire bat, you can bite me any time you like.' He winked at me, grin lascivious, making me uncomfortable. Simon was right about Savile, but it pushed the boundaries to come dressed as a notorious abuser.

Ten minutes later, Verity saw him. Her eyes narrowed as she stalked forward. She sneered, 'Slimy bastard, as well as a paedo, just right for your style.'

'You're looking lovely yourself, Verity,' he said. 'The wart suits you.' He laughed uncomfortably.

'My outfit's a joke, but dressing as Savile makes light of the appalling things that man did. It's in terrible taste. You're the sort who'd wear a Hitler costume. Don't you understand why it's objectionable? You are such a waste of space,' she replied.

The two glared at each other over the red glow of the bonfire. Ben and I watched the standoff, glanced at each other, then intervened in unison.

'Si, what track should we play to get this party going?' asked Ben

'Verity, someone's said they're gluten-free. You said there were buns somewhere, but I can't find them.' I took her arm and led her towards the kitchen.

'I hate him,' she said and blinked away a tear.

The Savile outfit was horrible, but equally Verity was as drunk as a skunk. I wasn't sure what to think about Simon. His conversation entirely related to himself and his interests. The signs were there in spades; I thought. It's crunch time. Did I carry on chasing a relationship with this, handsome, self-centred, sleazy guy or move on?

Verity made for the baby grand piano and played, 'House of the Rising Sun'. Mellow notes rippled through the room and out of the open bifold doors. The party gathered around, stopped talking and leant in to listen, her musicianship was sublime.

Ben came up and whispered an explanation. 'Vee is a jazz pianist. She has played with the best. Her career was taking off when we first met. She gave it up to move here. I wonder whether that's why…' His words trailed off and he swallowed. 'Why she seems to despise me these days.'

I wasn't sure what to say. Should I mention that his being away in London so much didn't help? That she complained about how he was always going out with Simon?

Verity continued playing, her audience rapt, and someone called for Bat Out of Hell. Soon we were bawling out Meat Loaf lyrics. I flapped my cape wildly. Everyone danced as Verity played on. Simon grabbed me and we jived, but his eyes, like everyone's, remained on the soloist.

As the party wound up, Simon said, 'Let's meet next week. I'll text you an evening when I'm free. What's your number?'

'Nah, I'm busy. We haven't much in common. I'll pass,' I said. The look of shock on his face gave me a thrill of pleasure. I didn't actually like anything about Simon. He was a creep and a two timing one at that. For once I'd acknowledged it before becoming entangled.

Drew

I stayed in London over the weekend; it was easier.
I'd seen the poster for the PTA Halloween party at the
Oaks on the village notice board. Amy would be there,
although she didn't have children either, and probably
with that Simon Evans. If she knew his reputation; that
he had loved and abandoned two partners locally, left
them with a baby each; she might not like him so
much. Would anyone have told her?

I woke to a misty Saturday morning and took a run
along the Thames, crunching through fallen leaves,
showered and, with nothing better to do, caught up
with work emails. Later, the sun shone and it was a
glorious afternoon. I picked up a novel, Beloved, I'd
been meaning to read for years.

A member of Chiswick House Trust, I used its
gardens regularly for runs and walks. I crossed over
the A4, through the gates and headed for the Italian
Garden and the conservatory. It was cordoned off; a
wedding. I walked on, but they'd shut off another
section around the marquee; yet another wedding.
Tourists and Londoners alike strolled in pairs or as
families, making the most of the late autumn sunshine.
It seemed as if I was the only person in the garden
unaccompanied, alone.

I found a secluded bench in the walled garden and
tried to read as the words swam before my eyes. I
couldn't settle or concentrate. Should I have a tea in
the cafe before it closed?

An elderly man in a blazer, leaning heavily on a stick, his back stiff and straight, shuffled up, and sat at the furthest end of my bench, the way everyone in London does. His short haircut and trimmed moustache suggested he was ex-army, a typical Chiswick resident. There were vacant benches elsewhere. I guessed he'd want to talk.

'Lovely afternoon,' he said.

'Isn't it?' I replied.

'My wife loved it here, especially the conservatory. Such a beautiful garden.'

'I tried to go in, but there was a wedding,' I replied.

'We married in Suez; fifty-one wonderful years.'

I had to be kind, but couldn't help thinking morosely that in fifty years, I'd be ninety, even if I married tomorrow.

'When did you lose your wife?' I asked.

'A year ago tomorrow and miss her every day. She was my soul mate, kept me on my toes, told me what to do and when.'

'I'm so sorry. Do you have children?'

'Two, but they have their lives to lead. It's not the same as having someone of your own.'

He shook himself. 'I don't mean to sound maudlin and spoil your day. We had a wonderful life together. I wouldn't exchange a moment. Now then must get on. I'm sure you have someone to get home to. I'll leave you in peace.'

He walked off towards the main house, leaving me lonelier than ever. In my mind's eye, I saw bloody Simon Evans drape his arm over Amy's shoulders. Was it too late to make her like me?

Chapter 11

Amy

A couple of weeks later, I'd returned from a
Monday morning shift in the village shop and settled
to work at my desk, when screeching brakes followed
by a dull thud sounded outside. I looked out of the
window. A white delivery van was stopped at the
junction of the lane to Rooks Row. I hurried out to see
what had happened.

A pathetic bundle of black and white fur lay to the
left of the van. I screamed, 'Hammy,' and ran towards
it as the driver turned a guilt riddled face towards me.

'I'm so sorry Miss, the dog came from nowhere,
honest.'

I knelt and realised with shocked relief it wasn't
Hamburger. It was old Meg. Blinking back tears, I
stroked, then lifted her head. Sightless eyes lolled at
me.

'From the sound of the brakes, you were going fast,
too fast,' I said.

He didn't reply directly.

'Shouldn't have been running loose, it's an offence.
Is it your dog? Would you like me to call the police?
We have to report accidents unless the owner tells us
not to. It's company policy.'

'No, she belongs to the farmer down the lane. We
have to tell him.'

'I'll put the body in the van.'

We knocked at the farm door. Mr Giles appeared and looked questioningly at us.

'It's Meg. She's had an accident,' I stammered.

'Your dog is in the back of the van,' added the driver.

Mr Giles limped over to the doors, which swung open to reveal poor Meg.

He collapsed into gasping, gulping sobs. Hammy ran up and nuzzled at Meg's remains, whining miserably.

The driver lifted the old dog's corpse onto the grass by the door, then helped Mr Giles into the house. 'I'm very sorry, but I have to go,' he said. 'I'll lose my job if I've late deliveries. Sir, your dog walked into the van, instead of away from it, I'm afraid. '

I knew better than to argue with the man. Delivery drivers are under huge time pressures. 'OK, you get on with your round. I'll make us a cup of tea, then I'll ring his son.'

Even after I'd made him tea, Mr Giles continued to cry. I'd expected him to be upset, but not this.

Eventually, he spoke. 'Meg is, I mean was, old. Her eyesight and hearing had gone. She may have got disorientated and walked into the van. I've been talking with Drew about whether to get the vet to put her down these last couple of months. She's at peace and I envy her. Only wish someone would run me over; put me out of my misery.'

Tears trickled down his chin.

'Mr Giles, can I ring Andrew. Ask him to come home?'

'Don't bother the lad, he's busy.'

'He'll want to know, won't he? I asked. Do you have his number?'

'I suppose so. He'll be at work, in meetings. I use his office number in the daytime.'

He called out a London number, which I tapped out into my phone, then I stepped outside for privacy.

'Giles and Harding, Andrew Giles' office here. How can I help?' came a silky-smooth voice down the line.

'Hello, my name is Amy Stuart. I need to speak to Andrew urgently.'

'Amy, yes Mr Giles has mentioned you,' she said.

Not another person hearing about the marrow; I sighed internally. My exploit was entertaining offices in London now.

'It's his father's dog. There's been an accident. Could you find him urgently, please?'

'Of course, his conference call has just finished.'

I heard her press a button and speak down another line.

Drew's voice came on the line. 'Amy? What's happened? What has Jet done now?'

'I'm ringing about Meg. A van ran her over, she's dead. I'm worried about your father. He hasn't stopped crying since we told him.' I dropped my voice. 'He said he wished he could be put out of his misery, too.'

'Oh, no, Meg's been Dad's shadow for the last twelve years. He'd always have been upset, but he's so low right now, I'm not that surprised. I'll have to insist he sees the doctor. Thank you so much for ringing, Amy; for being there for him.'

'No problem. It happened at the turning to the farm, outside my cottage. I was right there, heard it all.'

'I'll cancel my meetings and leave at once. It will be some time until I get back from London; the traffic won't be great this time of day. Would you... would you mind staying with him for a few hours?'

'Not at all, but is there no one he knows better?'

Andrew sighed wearily. 'No one. He's refused to socialise since the stroke. Won't go out, says he's an embarrassment, even before that... Anyway, I'm sorry to ask, but would you sit with him?'

I returned to the farmhouse to tell Mr Giles his son was on his way.

Sharp eyes stared at me. 'He's asked you to watch me, hasn't he? You don't need to. I'll be fine. It was the shock talking. I didn't mean it, the way it sounded. I'm not going to harm myself.'

'I have to stay, I promised Drew. he said,Meg's been a friend to you for twelve years. You're bound to be upset. Where shall we sit? The kitchen? Tell you what, I'll make supper for you both; it's a long drive from London. Drew will be hungry when he gets back.'

Mr Giles snorted, but led me into a large kitchen. I'd never been in the room before and it wasn't what I expected; with a clotted cream coloured Aga and matching, painted bespoke cabinets, a Belfast sink and a double oven, microwave and American fridge freezer with a huge, marble-topped central island.

'Your kitchen is amazing.' It was the wrong thing to say.

He launched into a tirade. 'Bloody nonsense is what it is. That woman designed it before she left.

Nothing wrong with the old one, I told her. It was good enough for Drew's grandparents and me, but she insisted. I agreed in the end to stop the nagging.

'Two months later she up and left my son; not that I ever saw her cook. I kept the old dresser in the pantry. I miss seeing my grandparents' colourful crockery out on the shelves. They collected Welsh Gaudy, it brightened the place up. Not like this beige paint, Mole's Back and Smoked Trout. What kind of colours are those?'

His arm waved at the room. 'The oak table has gone into the barn. My family ate around that table for hundreds of years.'

Hammy ran in and settled into a dog basket beside the Aga without making a sound.

Distracted, Mr Giles said, 'He and Meg shared a bed.' Tears seeped down his cheeks. I didn't know what to do or say. After a while, he stopped, sniffed, and said. 'I'm a daft old fool. I'm sorry, Amy. What must you think of me? I never cry. These last couple of years, everything's got on top of me.'

I had to change the subject, get him talking about something positive. In desperation I asked, 'What line of work is Andrew in? What do Giles and Harding do?'

'They are architects, very successful ones. Drew's made a real go…' He stopped. I hadn't quite let out a sneer or scoffed, but my face gave me away.

'You don't approve?'

'No, of course, it's an excellent job. Where I worked last though, architects could be absolute pains, so difficult.'

'What did you do?'

His face showed interest. I'd stopped him thinking about Meg. Only now I had to tell him about my problems.

I sighed. 'Until five years ago I was an archeologist; worked for Wessex Archeology. It was my dream job. I loved it there. We taught students on placement and completed excavation surveys for developers and architects.'

'Drew doesn't speak kindly about you lot. He had a major bust with some a few months back, in fact. Why did you leave?'

'Money, why else? Alan, he is my ex, said I'd earn more using my IT skills. That we'd get a bigger mortgage. He was right... but.'

'But?'

'I miss it. I loved my work. Yes, even the arguments with architects and developers. It fascinated me, still does. Understanding who and what went before us. My current job is fine, the people there are nice. That's the but.'

Mr Giles nodded slowly. 'In my experience, you should follow your dreams. Otherwise, you end up old and riddled with regrets about what might have been.'

'Your experience?'

'I gave up on University and other things because of money, responsibilities. I farmed as my father did before me.'

'But it's so lovely here and the farm's well run.'

'It is beautiful, but farming's a hard life, and lonely.'

Damn, I'd got him back talking about his unhappiness. What should I do to distract him?

'I said I'd cook. What have you got in the fridge? Anything we can stew?'

'Lots, I've a chest freezer full of best Welsh Black beef, all from my fields. It needs using up.'

'You'll have to show me how to use the Aga. I saw apples falling from a tree in your garden. How about a crumble and custard for pudding?'

He searched under the sink and produced a tatty plastic carrier bag. 'Best I show you the orchard; point out which trees produce the best cookers.'

Hammy and I followed him to a large fenced enclosure behind the farmhouse, with dozens of apple and pear trees. The ones nearest the house were younger, but in the distance I saw hunched ancient trees covered with lichen, moss and laden with mistletoe and apples.

He waved his arms towards the newer trees. 'I planted these thirty years ago; they are mostly cider apples. Did it as the bottom fell out of the cider market.' He scoffed, but had a smile, as he remembered.

'Cider is all the rage these days. I guess you'd be able to sell them now.'

He nodded. 'I've wondered about that myself. Even considered making it myself. Thought I might ask around. There is local cider in the farmer's market. Course hundreds of years ago it was all everyone drank around here and in Herefordshire. Apples grow better than hops, and barley was expensive.'

He pointed at two trees nearby. 'Those are cooking apples; Bramley's, but my grandmother's favourite, is down at the bottom of the orchard. She always said

Lord Derby had the best flavour, it's an early, so better for a crumble right now.'

He enjoyed pointing out the different varieties to me. Under a stand of pear trees, he stopped again. 'I remember my father planting these when I was ten; pears for heirs, he told me. They'll be Drew's in time. After that,' he shrugged.

'There's loads of mistletoe on the old trees at the end. Perhaps I could take some to the village shop to sell nearer Christmas?'

'Of course you can. Drew used to pick it when he was a lad. He'd take bundles back to Cardiff with him. I assumed it was for him and his mates to kiss girls under, but no. Turned out he was selling it to florists and peddling it himself outside the market and he made a decent sum each year. His mother said the boys spent it on drink and told me off.' Mr Giles grinned at the memory. 'He was always sharp, my Andrew.' He glanced at me. 'Got a heart of gold, though. I know he seems standoffish. He's shy around women, that's all.'

He stopped again under a tree laden with large green apples. 'Let's choose some Lord Derby's for our crumble.'

Back inside the house, sitting near Meg's basket, the farmer became morose again, lost in his thoughts. When Drew turned up three hours later, I was pleased to see him. Solid and reliable in a smart dark suit and tie. He didn't seem dull at all; he looked organised and dependable. His father's words came back to me, "Got a heart of gold."

Drew

Angel buzzed, 'Sorry to disturb you, but there's a Miss Stuart on the phone for you. Something about your father's dog. She insisted it was urgent.'

What had that puppy got up to now? Why was Amy contacting me at work?

'Very well, put her through.'

'Amy? What's happened? What's Jet done?'

Tone anxious, she told me old Meg had been run over, and explained she was worried about Dad. He'd told her he wished he was dead and was uncertain if it was safe to leave him by himself.

Who could I ask to go in? I knew the answer; Dad had been a recluse since the stroke. There was Selwyn, but with his tactlessness he'd make things worse. I'd no choice. I'd have to ask Amy if she'd stay until I got there. Luckily she agreed, didn't make a fuss, said it was no trouble. Something about her had convinced me she wasn't the kind to let anyone down.

Angel sorted out my diary; most meetings were cancelled, delayed or could be held by conference call, but Helsinki was unavoidable. 'I'll drive straight to the airport from Brecon on Wednesday.' I told her, 'and then home on Friday. Could you ask Daniel to go to the Essex meetings for me?'

As I mentioned Daniel's name, she smiled to herself. Ah ha, has the ice maiden begun to melt? I wondered.

I drove home, wondering how Dad would be. Expected to have to cajole him to do anything; change his clothes, eat, let alone see the GP. When I finally got in, the delicious smell filling the kitchen was a surprise, as was the sight of Dad's hair dusted with flour. Had he cooked?

The expression of relief on Amy's face when I arrived was almost funny. She grabbed her cosy fleece jacket and was on her way out before I could thank her.

As she left, she turned to Dad and said, 'Forecast is set fair for tomorrow. Will I see you and Hammy at the turning, as usual?'

His response was gruff. 'Of course, one o'clock sharp.'

Had they been meeting often? Did he let her call Jet, Hammy?

On the drive back I'd set up an urgent appointment for Dad at GP surgery for the next morning. I didn't tell him, decided it'd be better to say next morning, rather than argue all evening.

At 4 am, a noise below my bedroom woke me. Bleary-eyed, I stumbled downstairs. There he sat in grubby pyjamas, hunched in the chair by the Aga, face set grim and sad.

'What's wrong?'

'Nothing, couldn't sleep. Never can these days.'

'You are depressed, you know that, don't you?'

He sighed. 'I do. Everything seems pointless. I can't see a future. I've failed you, Andrew.'

'Failed me, in what way?'

'I set a bad example divorcing your mother. Look at the mess of your marriage. It was my fault, he said.'

'No, it wasn't. I was stupid not seeing through Steph sooner. Everyone else did, believe me. My colleague Sally tried to warn me. I was blind to it.'

'I never liked her, but of course I didn't say so. It would have driven a wedge between you and me. First time she visited, she sized this place up. I could see her wanting it, but not to live in, to change.'

'Sorry about the kitchen, Dad, I know you miss your furniture. I should have been firmer with Stephanie, but she'd have sulked for weeks.'

'The woman planned to start on my lounge next. Had the alterations mapped out; told me we'd have big glass doors opening onto a terrace, and that it would brighten the place up no end! The sitting room wall faces due west; gales would have blown the glass in.' He hesitated then said, 'I am to blame though, that you had a broken home.'

'Dad, that is the depression talking. I had everything I needed from you and Mum, love and support. I've booked appointment to see the doctor tomorrow at eleven. You need help.'

He didn't argue, just shrugged, then asked, 'Will we be back in time to meet Amy with the dog? I said I'd see her at one.'

'Yes, don't worry.'

After a long wait in the GP surgery next day, we joined a long queue at the chemists to collect his new prescription.

Dad said, 'Let's get back, I'll be late for Amy. You come in and collect the tablets later.'

'Dad, it's a ten mile round trip. They'll be ready in a moment.'

95

We got home with fifteen minutes to spare. He got out of the car and set off down the lane, Jet in tow, the second we stopped.

Chapter 12

Amy

Tuesday lunchtime, the day after Meg's accident Aunt Jen's landline rang, an unknown number; probably a telesales worker wanting to sell me something.

It was Drew.

'Hello Amy, you left before I could thank you properly yesterday. It was very kind of you to stay with Dad.'

'No problem. I was glad to help. How's he doing?'

'I took him to his GP this morning. He started him on antidepressants, then offered a referral to a counsellor.'

I suppressed a giggle. 'I imagine the suggestion of talking therapy didn't go down well?'

'You're right. Told the doctor he wasn't baring his soul to anyone, thank you very much. He'd have tablets or nothing.'

There was a pause as he took a breath. 'I wondered if, whether I could take you out for a meal tonight and maybe to the pictures.' He gulped again. 'To say thank you.'

'There's no need. It's what neighbours are for. I've discovered one of the many nice things about living here, is you know your neighbours.'

Drew told me he'd like to take me, anyway. Was he asking me out on a date? My thoughts raced. This was unexpected. I wasn't certain he liked me. Surely it

97

was a thank you. Should I accept? There again, another night of watching soaps alone was the alternative. The pictures, what an old-fashioned way of putting it, that was Drew all over, gentlemanly and I couldn't help but admit, rather sexy.

'Oh, I guess I am free. OK, that'll be, ah, nice.'

'Pick you up at six?'

'Great. See you then.'

Drew

I plucked up my courage and rang to see if Amy wanted to go out. She might refuse, especially if she was still seeing Simon Evans. We'd always keep her aunt's number in case of any problems. My mouth dried up. I felt like a teenager, stumbling over the words. Dating apps are so much easier. Then again, I'd never minded whether the women said yes or no.

Naturally, I messed it up. Implied I was offering dinner as a thank-you for staying with Dad after the van ran over Meg. Stupid, stupid, why was I so bad at this?

Amy said no, of course, and that she was happy to help. I almost hung up, but made myself try again.

'I didn't mean only to thank you. I wondered, um, hoped we might go out. Are you free tonight?'

She sounded surprised, then cautious, but agreed in the end. She wasn't overly enthusiastic.

I checked what movies were on in Hay and Brecon. Top Gun; Maverick in Brecon, that didn't sound right, not a girl's film. Hay cinema is nicer, with plush comfortable seats and a bar. There was a rom com on, one I'd never heard of and not my kind of movie, but maybe Amy would like it. I booked two tickets for the eight p.m. showing.

Dad was downstairs.

'I'm going out tonight.'

'Where are you off, the pub?'

I coughed, 'Offered to take Amy out. Thought a meal, then the cinema. Not sure where to eat, though.'

'Amy, ha, I thought you fancied her from the start. I can see why. She's an attractive woman. I like her. Be nice, not too stuffy.'

I raised my eyebrows, dating advice from my father. What was worse, he thought I could be stuffy with women, oh God!

I was ready by ten to six. Dad's eyes narrowed when I came down. 'Tweed jacket, going somewhere posh?' he asked.

'Not really, I tried to make a reservation, but it's short notice. The tapas bar in Hay doesn't take bookings and we're early, so should get a table, otherwise it's a pub.'

He scoffed. 'Huh, not so romantic; you should have booked sooner. Never mind, have a good evening. Give the girl my regards, say thank you from me. Don't mess the date up and shut the back door as you leave or Jet will join you. If he thinks you're with Amy, he'll want to come; he adores her.'

As I left, he shouted, 'Fill up the coal scuttle before you go. It's empty.'

I stepped on the brakes outside Well Cottage. Amy appeared in a cosy red coat with a hood the moment I got out of the car. I held open the passenger door, and we set off. I'd no idea what to talk about. What would interest a pretty IT worker?

She broke the silence to ask about my work. Nervous, by the time we'd parked in Hay, I'd given her my career highlights, but hadn't asked a single question about her life. To my relief, the tapas bar, in what had been The Red Lion, buzzed with customers. We sat at the last empty table beside a crackling log fire.

She took off her coat to reveal shapely legs in thick black tights under a leather miniskirt and rollback jumper.

'You look nice,' I said.

'Thanks, you look, um, smart,' she said. I saw her take in my jacket and cords. Had I dressed too staidly? I guessed so, from her response.

'This place seems fun; Spanish sharing plates. What shall we pick? I'm vegetarian, but choose meat dishes for yourself'

As we waited for our food, instead of looking me in the eye, Amy kept staring over my shoulder and to the side. Did she know someone behind us?

Before the waitress arrived to take our order, she took a breath. 'Um, Drew,'

'Yes?'

'You've a grimy smear all down one cheek. It's a bit distracting. Can I wipe it off for you?'

I groaned, 'It's dust from the coal shed, sorry.'

Laughing, she shook her head, leant towards to my face, then dabbed at the sooty mark with a tissue she'd moistened with a lick. My mouth dried at her closeness, at her tongue licking the tissue. I had to make a joke.

'Could be worse, I suppose. There's no spinach between my teeth, is there?'

'No, you're good; you won't scare the waitress.'

'How are you finding Talwern? Is the working from home OK? I did it after Dad's stroke but that was before broadband fibre reached the village. I guess it's easier now?'

'I love it. Everyone has been so welcoming.' She looked pensive. 'I'm considering emigrating, though. Not sure if you'd heard that my company is based in Melbourne? My boss has offered to sponsor me. As I've worked for an Australian company for 5 years, I'm eligible for a work visa.'

My heart stood still. She might leave and travel to the other side of the world. 'Don't do that. Talwern would miss you.' I attempted to keep my voice light.

A shadow passed over her face. 'I've been living here for nearly three months, and Aunt Jen gets home in February. I'm going to have to make up my mind soon,' she said. 'Should I try to buy somewhere in Bristol or not? I've considered looking around here. My money would go a lot further. I could buy a house with a garden in Brecon for the price of a two bedded flat in Bristol. But then again, if I move to Australia, buying a property in the UK would be a mistake.' She grimaced. 'I've no idea where I'm going with my life.'

I leant forward and took her hand. 'Don't feel bad, neither do I. After my divorce, the ground shifted. I've nowhere to put roots, I'm lost.'

'Me too,' she sighed.

101

We were still holding hands. I stroked her thumb. It was time for honesty.

'I'm glad you came tonight. I've been thinking about you since, well ever since the exploding marrow. I'm hopeless at dating, always was. Could have kicked myself for suggesting it was a thank-you.'

Her eyes met mine, and she squeezed my hand. She glanced at her watch. 'The film starts in ten minutes. Hadn't we better leave?'

When we got to the cinema, I said, 'Damn, the back row's full.'

'Maybe next time?' When she smiled up at me, my heart did a somersault.

I longed to kiss her but made do with holding her hand through one of the stupidest films I've ever had the misfortune to watch. I didn't care. Holding her hand in the dark was enough. As the film ended, before the lights turned up, I couldn't resist. I pulled her palm to my mouth and kissed the inside of her wrist. Felt her shiver as my tongue licked her pulse point. Then I remembered about Simon Evans. Was Amy dating both of us?

Amy

When Drew came, he jumped out and opened the passenger side door. It was lovely being treated as if I mattered. To break the ice, I asked about his work and we were soon chatting about his pet projects. I worried he might get on to archaeological surveys, but apart from mentioning newts once, nothing came up. He'd made it pretty clear it was a date to thank me for looking after his dad. It wasn't worth spoiling our evening by telling him about my old profession. His father obviously hadn't mentioned my earlier career.

He took me to a charming, low beamed bar. The staff were amazing, so friendly, and made us feel like regulars. No wonder the bar was filled with cheerful people of all ages, laughing and drinking. Drew helped me take off my jacket, and complimented my outfit.

He was in his usual tweed and cords combo. I'd always thought they looked comfortable, if predictable, but they suited him. I couldn't imagine Drew wearing anything else. When I noticed a smudge of soot on his right cheek, I couldn't decide whether to mention it. He was nervous and admitted he found dating difficult. The longer I left telling him, the harder it became. It repeatedly drew my eyes back. Drew looked over his shoulder twice because of my stares.

Eventually, I gave up and told him. He blushed as I wiped the mark off. As I touched his cheek, my heart quickened; he was kind of cute with those helpless brown eyes.

The chef had to love Spain or be Spanish, because the tapas dishes tasted as if they'd come from Malaga. There were loads of veggie choices, which is unusual; the aubergine and chickpea stew was great and Drew said his chorizo in local cider was delicious as we dug into a shared patatas bravas and a goats cheese and honey salad.

As we left the restaurant, he pulled me towards him protectively while we walked the hundred yards to the little cinema. It was pretty, with a tiny bar serving glasses of wine or local gin. There were forty or so tan leather armchair seats, with a drinks holder between. Very civilised, nothing like the big screens I watched as I kid. Drew was driving, and offered me an alcoholic drink, but I settled for a lemonade. I couldn't get the memory of my drunken ladder escapade away and hoped to prove I wasn't a dipsomaniac.

'I haven't been to the movies for ages,' I whispered. The film was pleasant nonsense, but holding Drew's hand was lovely. When the guy got the girl as it finished, Drew gave the inside of my wrist a slow kiss. My heart pounded; it was sexy, tantalising.

He walked me to the door of Well Cottage and then pulled me close. My legs turned to jelly. I had to wrap my arms around his neck to hold myself upright. When he kissed me a second time, I didn't want him to stop, but he stepped back after long moments.

'Coffee?' I offered.

His face looked regretful.

'Better not, there's the car outside and I'm up at five tomorrow. I've a few chores for Dad and then a plane to catch from Heathrow to Finland at eleven on Wednesday. Can we do this again when I get back? Friday?'

'I'm going home to my parents in Somerset for an early Christmas celebration after working in Bristol on Friday. They are in New Zealand for all of December, visiting Aunt Jen and Diane. I was invited, but, thought I'd go another time. In case I decide to try Australia.'

He raised his eyebrows with a mock grimace, then pulled out his phone to look at his diary. 'I'm speaking in a conference in Dublin the next weekend, and have late meetings on the following Friday, so two weeks on Saturday? I'll book somewhere. The end of November is getting close to Christmas party season, we won't get a table otherwise.'

'Sure,' I replied, deflated. 'I'll pop in and see your father each day too, make sure he's OK.' Why didn't Drew want to come in? So much for passionate kisses. Had he taken me out to thank me for helping with his dad, after all?

Chapter 13

Amy

I kept up my regular runs with Hamburger. Over the next two weeks, Mr Giles appeared out working around the farm more often. He was whistling one day when I returned, hot and sweaty with his dog.

He shuffled his feet and looked at his wellington boots. 'Thanks all you did that day with Meg, Amy. Sorry I cried. It must have embarrassed you.'

'It was not a problem. When it happened, for a second I thought it was Hammy under the van, and I could hardly bear it. I'd have cried. You've had Meg for years. I've only known Hammy for a couple of months.'

'I've been thinking about what you said about missing archeology,' he said. 'Did you know there are the remnants of a medieval village in the fields behind the farm? Been told they abandoned it at the time of the Black Death. I can show you sometime. If, if you like?' He looked uncertain and my heart went out to him.

'I had no idea, and I'd love to. That is really interesting. I'll look up what they have found online tonight.'

He was right. I searched Coflein, the Ancient Monuments' website, it listed the details of the site. How hadn't I noticed the sunken paths that crossed my run routes? Holloways, they were a sure sign of ancient settlements. The website suggested that

Talwern had been one of the largest medieval villages in the region.

Mr Giles's mood kept on improving. He smiled more, chatted easily, and occasionally laughed with me before my runs. One sunny morning when we met at the top of the lane, he wore a waxed jacket and walking boots.

'Grand winter's day. Thought instead of you running today, we could explore that ancient village I told you about? You can show me what to look for. Pop home to get a coat. Your outfit is all right for running, but you'll get cold walking at my pace.'

He set off, arms waving enthusiastically, explaining all about the land that had been in his family for so many years.

'My grandfather started breeding Welsh Black cattle here, took a pride in them. Dad won prizes in local shows and built up the herd.'

'Has the area been ploughed frequently, do you know?'

'Not where we are going, because it's steep. The fields have been grassland, meadow, all my life and, as far as I know, my father and grandfather's, but most likely longer. Wait until you see the wildflowers in spring and early summer; yellow rattle, ragged robin, three types of orchids. My cattle loved the rich pasture; it fattened them up beautifully.'

His shoulders drooped. 'I improved the herd, bought better stock, and balanced traits. It was something thing I could do to make up for, for what, what I'd given up, university, and all that.Gave me back a sense of achievement, pride. My bulls won

107

best in show at the Royal Welsh four times and fetched top prices. Broke my heart to see them go after my stroke. But you can't mange cattle without muscle.'

I followed him up the sloped lane behind the church, worried that his disability would mean he wouldn't be able to walk. Skeletal branches touched above our heads; dense moss and lichens made the path feel timeless. Mr Giles managed well, with no sign of his limp as he marched ahead leading the way. The lane forked at the top. To one side, a metal five-barred gate opened into a field with a view out over the village to the lake and hills beyond.

The farmer gazed into the distance, lost in his own thoughts, whilst I scanned the field. There were six or seven flat areas that might be ancient building platforms. It'd be a good spot for a village, I thought and the cathedral in Brecon might hold some tithe records. I itched to find out more about the site.

Dotted around the field were red mounds of soil; dozens and dozens of mole hills.

Mr Giles kicked one. 'I'll call in the catcher in the spring. Trouble is, when you drive machinery, the mole runs can collapse. On a slope like this, a tractor could topple.'

'It's not uncommon for archeologists to use mole hill soil to survey for artefacts. Samples what's there, without digging trenches,' I said.

'Really? Never knew that. Let's have a look at a few shall we?'

It was his land. I might have said we needed to be systematic, and mark out grids, but I missed spending my summer at digs.

'OK. How about you try over by that flat spot? It looks a potential building platform. I'll look here.' I took a small trowel from my pocket and so did he.

'Great minds, eh? Popped it in my pocket on impulse.'

I giggled. 'Weird as it sounds, I never travel anywhere without one.'

My mole hills produced a good trawl of earthworms, but nothing more. Mr Giles gave a shout, and I hurried over.

He held out a pot sherd. 'What do you think of this?' He handed it to me.

'It is unglazed pottery, rough local clay at a guess, hard to say how old it is. The Back Death decimated Europe in 1348; pots were pretty basic back then, rare for them to be glazed. Are there any more shards?'

He scraped gently at the earth mound. Another larger piece emerged, miraculously the two fitted together.

I turned the pottery in my hand, rubbed off the mud, then gasped. 'I can't believe it. Look, put together they have decoration, it's a face. Can you see? There's an eye, nose and half a mouth.'

'Let me find my reading glasses.' He fumbled in his pocket, then peered at it. 'With a bit of imagination, I can make that out.'

'It wasn't uncommon for medieval pots to be decorated with humorous faces, but if it is 14th century, it will still be rare. I'll get the exact coordinates of the spot. We'll mark it in case the county archeologist is interested.' I checked the What3Words location and we stuck a hazel stick into the mole hill.

'I could take it in to the museum? It's not treasure, so it's yours, but if it turns out to be a medieval pot, they'll be interested.'

'I'll leave it to the experts, but I'd like to discover more. Do you think they'll want to do a dig? Like on Time Team.'

'Honestly, probably not. If this was an agricultural village without high status dwellings, there won't be much to discover. People owned very little back then, but the museum will log the find.'

He looked anxious as he asked, 'It wouldn't mean any restrictions on the site? Now and then, Drew and I talk about diversifying, planting a vineyard. This is a south facing slope and protected from the westerlies. I should have asked him to check about grants at that rural subsidies meeting in the Boar a month back.'

'I can't see a vineyard being an issue. It's not as if you want to build. It's agricultural land; you have every right to farm here. They might ask to explore whether the planting holes show anything of interest. Make a decent PhD project for a student. My PhD was in Roman glass.'

'You should be called Doctor Stuart by rights, then? You don't call yourself doctor?'

'Seemed no point once I left and started a new career. It made me feel old in the office and reminded me of what I'd abandoned.'

He looked at me with sympathy, then nodded. Mr Giles understood why I didn't like to be reminded of my old career. He'd given up college, and then lost his consolation, the Welsh Blacks. I changed the subject. No point in either of us dwelling on life's disappointments.

'A vineyard sounds interesting.'

'There's been a successful one in Abergavenny for years; Sugar Loaf wines. With global warming, there are more British vineyards established every year. Co-operatives to press the grapes are starting up. Money to be made and investment in the future. If I were younger…' His voice trailed off again.

'How many years would it take?'

' At least five years before I'd get any decent wine production.'

'So you'd only be sixty-five by the time you sold your first bottles?'

'Only?'

'My father is sixty-five, and he says his retirement's just begun. That he's another twenty years of living life to the full.'

'Huh, not sure about that.'

He looked surprised as he thought about what I'd said, and didn't dismiss it as he would have a short while ago.

'What time does Drew get back this week? I asked, trying to sound casual.

On Wednesday, the museum called, asking me to drop by to meet the county archeologist and discuss the pottery. The receptionist led me past visitors, into a small book lined back office. A man with wild curly greying hair and scruffy cargo pants walked in

111

grinning. Someone I'd recognise anywhere; Mick Postlethwaite, my old tutor, a junior lecturer in Exter Uni when I'd seen him last. He wrapped me in a bear hug.

'Amy, great to see you. As I read the find description and your name, I guessed it was you.'

'Mick, of all people. How's things with Sherry and what, your two girls?'

'We've three now; six, four and eight months, along with a ten acre small holding outside Sennybridge. It's fantastic. You must come over; Sherry would be thrilled if you did.'

We spent a happy hour discussing the pot and a possible test pit on the find spot. Then we talked about Exeter Uni, and why he'd left academia for a simpler life. It was very much Mick's style. His wife was such a love that I couldn't wait to visit. We set up a date between Christmas and the New Year. As I left his office, he threw a bombshell.

'Amy, there's a vacancy in the county service; for Monmouthshire and South Gwent; it covers Caerleon. You remember the amphitheatre and Roman baths? There is one day a week teaching in Cardiff Uni during term time. You were a brilliant lecturer and would be a perfect fit. I'd thought of texting you a month ago. You must be fed up with that bloody office job by now. Apply; the closing date is Friday. Join my team; money's rubbish, of course, but the pension's not bad!'

'Your team?'

'Yeah, I head the service.' He made a face. 'Got promoted a year ago. It helps subsidise the chickens and goats.' As I left he winked, then said, 'At the interview tell them how important public engagement is; highlight your social media skills, and that encouraging younger people to understand what we do will bring them into the museum. It'll help convince the lay panel member.'

I walked back to my car, pensive. That night, I read the job description. Mick hadn't been joking about the salary; it paid 12K a year less than Bristol. I filled out the online application form anyway and pressed the send button. Odds were I wouldn't be shortlisted. Steady jobs like that are popular. There again, I knew Mick well and the cameos from the drains of the Roman Baths and glass finds from Caerleon were spectacular. It would be a fantastic job.

Saturday afternoon, I went shopping in Brecon for supplies. The Christmas lights were up and in the square the town brass band played carols. Notes of Silent Night drifted around the old buildings as the place thronged with Christmas shoppers. I stopped to chat with several of the village shop regulars. Bristol was great at Christmas, but there was more of a sense of community and belonging here.

I'd spent the last two weeks remembering my date with Drew; his kisses and refusal to come in. His face and body had told me he'd wanted to. I agonised, but decided I'd ask him to Well Cottage for a meal, instead of us going out. He'd walk from the farm. There wouldn't be a car parked outside. If things went well, then maybe… I planned to call in to Rooks Row Saturday lunchtime, pick up Hammy for a run and invite Drew over then.

I hummed as I cooked butternut squash curry, with extra curry sauce for a chicken breast I'd grill later. I'd a jar of mango chutney and packets of pittas and poppadoms in the cupboard. The cucumber raita was better made fresh. It was cold outside, so when I changed into my running kit, I threw an old sweatshirt on top, then jogged around to the farm.

The farmer answered the door, smiling. Hammy appeared from nowhere, ready to leave.

'Hi, Mr Giles. How are you?'

'Not so bad. Where are you off today?'

'Round the lake, as usual. Would you call Drew? I'd like to invite him for supper tonight, as long as you can spare him.'

Drew appeared behind his father, but he wasn't smiling as I'd expected. He glowered at me.

'Buttering up my father again?'

'Pardon?'

'You heard me. Wanting access to our fields for a dig? Or is that a lie? Are you really a bloody archeologist?'

'What? I don't know what you're talking about.'

'Heard of his plans for a vineyard, have you? Fancy yourself making wine as my step-mother. I'll have you know the land's mine. You need my permission to do anything on it, including any surveys.'

I gaped at him. Why was he so angry? What ever did he mean, step-mother?

Mr Giles turned and hissed at him. 'Don't be so damned rude, Drew. You're talking absolute nonsense. Apologise at once. Amy came to invite you to supper.'

Drew didn't say a word in reply. I wanted the ground to swallow me up. What on earth was happening? Inviting him for a meal wasn't a good idea. I was desperate to get away.

'Seems he wouldn't,' I said. 'Come on, Hammy, let's go for our run.'

Drew

It had been a nightmare fortnight juggling meetings in Helsinki, the conference and two projects UK that had gone pear-shaped. One developer threatened to sue Giles and Harding, although it was his construction team at fault. Surveys delayed the other project. I considered staying in London and trying to sort things out, but I was longing to see Amy. I hadn't been able to get the memory of that doorstep kiss out of my mind. The thought of Dad depressed and alone pulled me back, too. Although, he'd appeared brighter when I'd rung him midweek.

Late on Friday, I drove home after my late meeting. As I passed through the village, a motorcycle with two riders roared the other way. Amy's place was in darkness. Was she off on a date with bloody Simon Evans and the pillion passenger on the bike?

Dad had a casserole of beef in beer ready in the Aga. The kitchen was clean; he'd opened a bottle of red and the table laid. He wore a fresh shirt and whistled, *When the saints go marching in*. It was a transformation.

After a few mouthfuls, he said out of the blue, 'I've been researching what vines might produce the best grapes, given the weather and conditions of the West fields above the house. I sent off a soil sample for analysis.'

'Have you? I thought we'd decided it was too long a lead in time before any profit.'

'We had, but now I can't manage cattle I need a new interest. I was talking to Amy about it a few days ago,' he said.

'What would Amy Stuart know about viticulture? Not a lot I imagine.'

'Doctor Stuart may not, but she agreed the slope of the fields was right when we went up there on Tuesday.'

'Doctor? What do you mean, doctor? You went to the West fields with her? Why?'

'I took her up to the ancient village. Amy has a PhD in archeology and was interested when I told her about it a while back. When we were there, I found parts of a pot that might be old in a mole hill soil, would you believe? She's taken them to the museum to see what they think.'

I couldn't stop myself. 'What, you've let an archeologist onto our land? My land, in fact. Grandpa left it in trust for me, remember? You're telling me Amy is an archeologist?'

'The trust says the land is for my use until I die, so don't take that attitude. I took Amy there because I chose to. Why shouldn't I?'

'Because archeologists are damn nuisances, that's why. What if I want to build, sell for infill development? It's close to the village. I might apply for planning permission at some point,' I said, my fury growing.

'Sell our fields and build? You've never mentioned that before. You're being difficult. I hoped to discuss planting vines with you tonight, but it's pointless. All you think about are bricks and mortar. Never mind archeologists; Amy said architects could be pains. I suspect she's closer to the truth. Sell the fields our family has farmed for generations? Build houses on them? Well, I never.'

We finished our meal in silence. My head buzzed. Selwyn had told me Amy worked in IT, social media or something ridiculous. That she was an archeologist with a PhD made no sense. Could it be true? She didn't look at all like the grubby trousered brigade I was used to dealing with at work. Architects a pain? Was that what she thought about me?

My anger smouldered all night and my imagination ran away with me. I came up with plot after plot. A woman had betrayed me, again. She'd befriended Dad for her own purposes. She was toying with us both.

When Amy came round on Saturday morning, I let rip. Told her what I thought of her. Warned her off. As I shouted, I watched her face, which reflected complete confusion. With a sickening jolt, I realised I done it again. Same as the first time we'd met. I'd jumped to the wrong conclusion. Suggesting she had plans to seduce my father seemed so stupid in the light of day. Dad and I watched as Amy and the dog ran off down the lane.

He turned and said, 'Have you lost your mind? What a thing to say! As if Amy would flirt with me.

She's young enough to be my daughter, for heaven's sake.'

'I, I, well I didn't know what to think. You seem to be friends and you don't have friends, Dad. And well, the fields…'

I sounded absurd.

Dad gazed at me. 'She'd come to ask you to supper. Ruined that invitation comprehensively, didn't you?'

I looked at my shoes and felt six years old.

'I guess so.'

His voice softened. 'Messing up with women runs in the family. Apologise, go into town. Buy the girl some flowers.'

'I will. I'll see her after her run, when she gets back.'

I felt ill, knew I'd behaved like a jealous fool. I drove into Abergavenny and bought the biggest bunch of roses available, then in Waitrose a bottle of Mercer rum. With a felt-tip pen, I changed the name to Marrow.

I was outside Well Cottage by five and knocked.

She opened the door. 'It's you.' Her tone was flat.

'I'm sorry, really sorry. I was an idiot earlier.' I thrust the roses towards her.

'Apology accepted, I guess, but I've had enough. Take away those flowers. It's not only you, it's every man I meet; here, Bristol, everywhere. That's it, you are clowns, all of you. I'm done.'

Her forlorn expression broke my heart.

'Look, I brought you marrow rum.' Juggling the flowers she'd rejected, I pushed the yellow labelled bottle at her. She shook her head.

'Drink it with your father. I mean it Drew, leave. I can't go through any of this rubbish again. You clearly hate archaeologists; well, in my view, architects are often pompous, money grubbing desecrators. You breed and eat meat; I'm a committed vegetarian. There's no future in any of this, is there? Bye.'

Not waiting for a reply, she closed the door in my face.

Chapter 14

Amy

The first week of December, the Met Office put out an amber weather warning for an approaching snow storm, along with stern advisories not to travel. Schools closed, they stood the volunteers down from the village shop and I arranged to work from home until it was safe to go in to Bristol. I woke next day to the snow. Icing sugar white dusting covered the garden and hills. It was lovely, what fun! I went and shook snow from Aunt Jen's tender plants.

After an early Zoom meeting, I checked my personal email. They had shortlisted me for the County Archeology service post; the interview scheduled for the fourth of January. Goodness, I wasn't sure what to do. My options were Australia and IT, an office job, or trying to go back to my career. I decided to talk it over with Mr Giles when I saw him; he'd understand.

I checked the Met Office website; it had upgraded the forecast. A red warning covered central Wales; a risk to life. At least a foot of snow, maybe more was expected over the next few hours. I shivered. Maybe it would not be such fun after all.

I made carrot, orange and harissa soup for lunch, perfect for the weather, then texted Mum in New Zealand to reassure her I was safe and hadn't ventured to Bristol. By eleven, two inches of snow covered the path, while an east wind howled down the chimney.

After my soup, I started work on the laptop. Persistent barking I recognised sounded from outside. I opened the door to let Hamburger in. He wouldn't come, kept running halfway down the path, expecting me to follow.

'I can't possibly take you for a walk in this, you silly dog. Come inside,' I called repeatedly.

He stood his ground, yapping, looking out to the gate, body as tense as a bowstring. I knew I'd have to go with him or he'd freeze. Grumbling, I grabbed Jen's warmest anorak and followed. He ran ahead through swirling snow, head turning, stopping every few yards to check I was behind. Just as well, the flurries were so thick, I could barely make his dark shape out. He shimmied under the gate into Rooks Row farm yard and waited. Once I was inside, the dog raced towards the barn, and barked again and again. Something felt very wrong. Hands and feet frozen, I had no choice but accompany him.

The barn door stood open. Inside, a blue tractor had toppled to one side, a hay bale carrier attached to the front tilted an angle. Pinned beneath the carrier, half under a huge round bale, was Mr Giles.

I swallowed and hurried over, chest hammering. The farmer lay unmoving, pale as a sheet. Kneeling, I put my hand on his brow. His skin felt ice cold; was he dead? I pulled away, horrified.

I held his wrist and tried to find a pulse. Nothing. Had the accident killed him? Hamburger came over and tugged at his owner's sleeve, pulling the cloth of the old tweed jacket.

121

'Stop that,' I ordered. The arm moved and the farmer's eyebrows flickered. He was alive, thank goodness.

'Mr Giles, Mr Giles, it's Amy from Well Cottage. What has happened?' He didn't respond.

Stupid question, I thought. Anyone could see that an enormous hay bale had fallen on him. I wondered whether to pull him out, but knew if his back was broken, it might be dangerous. I pushed at the bale, but attached to the carrier and the tractor, it didn't budge an inch.

I rummaged in my pocket for my mobile, dialled 999, and prayed there'd be signal. There was.

'Ambulance services please.'

A calm woman took my panicked call, as I explained what I'd found and where we were.

'Is the patient conscious?' she asked.

'No, and he's freezing cold.'

'Is the airway clear? Is he breathing?'

'Barely.'

'It's a situation red, but an ambulance won't be able to reach you by road,' she said. 'They are all backed up in A&E and anyway the roads into Powys are closed. I'll call out the air ambulance.'

'Please tell them to hurry. I'm not sure how long he'll last or how bad he is. I can't find a pulse.'

'Give me a moment to sort out the helicopter and then I'll talk you through first aid.'

I held the phone and shivered; bitterly cold, the ground must be frozen; no wonder Mr Giles was cold, possibly hypothermic.

What should I do? Who could help? With nearly a foot of snow piled by the barn door and the roads blocked, I was on my own. Hammy nudged my arm, then sat close to his owner.

The ambulance call centre came back on to the phone. 'They've scrambled the Welshpool helicopter. It is on its way and will reach you in 25 to 35 minutes. Is the patient responding at all?'

'He's moved once, so he is alive, but he's barely breathing and he's so cold. The barn is freezing.'

'Cover him. Find a hot water bottle and blankets,' she said.

I looked around. Neat and tidy, there were no coverings in the barn, not even an old sack. 'I'll have to go into his house.' I replied.

'Do that. I'll wait on the line.'

Hammy paced beside us. 'Stay, sit,' I said. Hamburger lay on the ground next to his owner. I put the man's arm over the dog's hind leg. Like a living hot water bottle, I thought. I left the phone and ran outside, nearly slipping. The farm door was barely visible in the blizzard. What if it was locked?

To my relief, the back door handle turned, and I went through into the kitchen. The Aga in the chimneypiece had the kettle warming on top. I raced upstairs, pulled a duvet off a bed and, as an afterthought, a pillow and ran back to the kitchen. I'd never find a hot water bottle. What else was there? In a kitchen drawer I found zip-lock bags and half filled one with water from the tap, topped it up with hot water from the kettle and rushed back out into the snow. The chill hit me like a hammer as I left the kitchen.

I wrapped the duvet around his body, then slipped the pillow under his head. He moaned as his eyes flickered open. I heard a mumble. 'My leg, it hurts.' His eyes couldn't focus.

'What's happening? Where am I?' he asked.

'It's Amy, Mr Giles. You're in your barn. The tractor toppled onto you. The ambulance is on its way.'

He shook his head, and said, 'I was going to feed the sheep; blizzards are forecast.' He lapsed into silence, drifted back to into unconsciousness.

The call handler's voice came through my phone. 'Did I hear the patient speak?'

'Yes, but he's stopped now.'

'Don't let him fall asleep. Rouse him, keep him talking,' she said. 'The paramedics have given an ETA of fifteen minutes. Not long now. Try to keep him awake.'

'Thanks.' I pulled at Mr Giles's arm and Hamburger licked his face.

What could I say? I thought about my escapade with the broken key. 'Mr Giles, do you remember Andrew going up the ladder back in October?' I asked. 'You told him he had to take his trousers off. It makes me laugh every time I think about it.'

His lips formed a faint smile.

'Tell me about when Andrew was young. Has he always helped on the farm?'

'Holidays. He loved it here, but his mother insisted he went to school in Cardiff.'

'Had you divorced?'

124

'The life of a farmer's wife isn't for everyone.... it is lonely.'

'I guess it can be isolated. How did you meet?'

'I married on the rebound, whirlwind romance. Jane hated winters here. People in the village.... weren't kind either, nor were my parents. I never forgave them for that. Andrew was the only good thing to come of our marriage.'

'Your ex-wife lived in Cardiff, then?'

'Lives, yes, she does. Jane went back there after four years of trying. Couldn't blame her. It was my fault. There was somebody before, somebody I truly loved. Our families were against it. I should have stood up to them. Told them the past wasn't our problem.'

His eyes closed and seemed on the verge of falling into unconsciousness. I had to keep him talking.

'Why were you going out in the snow?' I asked.

He started. 'The sheep, they're in the top field. I have to bring them down.' He attempted to move, but gave a cry of pain.

In the distance, rotor blades purred; the helicopter had arrived.

'They'll be all right. The snow will soon melt.' I tried to sound hopeful.

'No, sheep die. They'll suffocate in snow drifts by the look of the weather. Seen it often. Freeze to death, like I would have if you hadn't come.' He shuddered.

Two paramedics and a doctor appeared at the door. In a flurry of activity, they worked out how to move the tractor and hay bale. Two of them used a plank as a lever and lifted it six inches to allow the doctor to pull him free. He looked no weight as they manoeuvred him onto the stretcher.

Mr Giles glanced over at me. 'Ring Drew, he'll look after everything.' He hesitated, then asked, 'Would you tell Gwen Havard something for me, in case,' he took a breath, 'in case I don't make it?'

I nodded.

'Tell Gwen I always loved her and that I'm sorry. I should have waited for her to come home.'

'I'll do it as soon as I can. Take care. Andrew needs you,' I said, my voice breaking. He looked so pale and frail.

The hum of the helicopter faded into the flat grey afternoon sky. Snow fell, fat flakes whirling ever faster. Chilled through to my bones, I hurried inside to warm beside the Aga before risking the three hundred yards walk home, then dialled the number of Andrew's office.

They connected me to the same PA as last time.

'Giles and Harding here. How can I help?'

'I need to speak to Andrew urgently again. It's Amy Stuart here.'

'Ah, Ms Stuart, I'm afraid Mr Giles is out of the county on business. I can leave him a message for Monday?'

'No, you don't understand. The air ambulance has taken his father into hospital. I have to speak to him. Please tell Drew his father's seriously injured, and to call me.'

'Oh no, that's terrible, I'll ring his mobile at once. If there is no service I'll get the Finland team to find him and get back to you.'

I made a pot of tea, then found dog biscuits for Hammy. He deserved a treat; he was a hero. Hamburger wolfed them down, went to the door, and barked repeatedly. He ran to me and then back to the door.

'Do you need to go?' I asked. 'Be quick then.' Hamburger trotted to the doorstep, waited, and whined over and over again.

'You want me with you? OK, I need to get home, anyway.' I put my coat and gloves on and, glancing at the falling snow, borrowed a grey bobble hat hanging on the back of the door. On impulse, I pulled a hooked shepherd's staff from the coat rack. It would stop me from slipping.

Hamburger yapped and ran in the opposite direction to Well Cottage. What did he want? There were only fields further up the lane? With a sinking heart, I realised he expected me to round up the sheep. He could herd, but a dog can't open farm gates. Around us lay drifts feet deep, but the snow wasn't falling as fast as earlier. I trudged behind him with difficulty. Opening the four gates was slow work, almost impossible; the bolts frozen into the wooden gateposts. Each took an age. I didn't close them behind us, left them ready for the sheep. Could we possibly herd the flock down the mountain alone?

After half an hour, we reached the top field; only common land and the gaunt mountaintops stood above us. The sheep gathered together in huddles, still as statues beside a hedge, which gave them scant shelter from the biting easterly, roaring down the hillside. To my relief, the top of a bag of sheep nuts poked above the snow outside the last gate, out of reach of the flock. Sheep invariably run towards a farmer shouting and shaking a feed bag. Maybe Hammy and I working together could manage to bring them down to the far.

I called out and shook a handful of nuts onto the ground outside the field, whilst Hammy bounded through the snow and driving them sheep towards me.

Once they smelt the food they moved, shaggy and dirty white, clumps of snow on their fleeces spraying everywhere as they pushed through pristine snow. Hammy stopped by a deep snowbank in the corner of the field and barked.

I balanced the bag of feed on a hedge out of reach of the sheep and staggered over to the him. There was nothing to be seen, but when I poked my stick into the drift, a muffled bleat emerged. There was an animal in there, buried under the snow. While I used the hook to clear out a path, my phone rang. I swore, took it out and yelled into it, 'Hello, who's there?'

'It's Andrew. Angel told me Dad's ill?' The wind whipped his voice away.

'Andrew, he had an accident.' I shouted. ' I found him in the barn. They have airlifted him to Cardiff. Could you ring the hospital as soon as possible? We're snowed in. I can't do anything to help.'

'Where are you? Why is the wind howling? I can barely hear you.'

'Hamburger and I are bringing the sheep down from the top field. Your father was headed up here before the tractor fell on him,' I yelled.

'The tractor fell? You're up on the mountain, in a blizzard? Alone?'

'Hamburger's with me.'

'Leave the damn sheep and get down off the mountain right now. There's a severe weather warning. They've cancelled flights back to the UK, leaving me stuck in Finland. For God's sake, get down off the hills.'

'We're going. Ring the hospital. I'll speak to you later,' I said.

I hung up, and gave a desperate poke at the drift, as snow began to fall once more. I broke open a gap wide enough to allow the sheep out. The herd and Hamburger rocketed down the slope as I stumbled through ever deeper snow, following in their wake. Walking down a half mile should have taken twenty minutes, but it took almost an hour to get back to Rooks Row.

I tried to leave the sheep in the closest field to the farm. Hammy was having none of it. He wanted them in the yard. The flock headed for the barn. Too cold and exhausted to attempt to close the door behind them, I let them go and collapsed onto the chair by the Aga, unable to move or think about going home. My phone had four WhatsApps and two texts from Andrew, asking if I was OK, the last two in capitals.

I texted, *Back at Rooks Row. Snow too deep to get home*, and pressed the send button, thinking I'd explain later. It was the first time we'd communicated after the row over archeology. I wasn't certain what we'd say to each other, but with his father was seriously ill, I couldn't refuse to speak. Hammy curled up on my feet. In the warmth, my eyelids got heavier, and I fell asleep, disturbed by jumbled dreams.

When I woke, it was dark, very dark. Wincing at the pain shooting down my back from sleeping in a chair, I flicked on the light switch; nothing. Power cut. I looked at my phone. It was eight a.m. and it should be daylight. What was going on? Snow covered the kitchen window and blocked all light from the room. When I tried the back door, it wouldn't budge.

I hurried to the other side of the house; the windows, although coated in slow flakes, let a cold light filter through. I pulled up the sash and stared out, only to hurriedly close it again in the glacial draft. I tested the front door. It moved two inches as I pushed, so I gave a heave and it swung open with a jolt. At least I wasn't trapped inside Rooks Row. Snow drifts filled the valley, every east facing slope piled high with powder, the road invisible after the storm. There was no way back to Well Cottage for the present. I checked my phone for charge, only twenty percent left. The cold must have drained it yesterday. When I tried the land line, it was dead.

No power meant no heat. When would the lines be repaired? It might be days until the electricity came back. Hell, whatever should I do? I examined the Aga; opened the chrome hotplate covers. One had a middle section with a hook. I lifted it up with a poker and peered down into the furnace. Dull grey embers sat at the bottom. It looked as if it might go out at any moment. A half empty coal scuttle stood to the stove, but throwing cold coals on to a fire would put it out. I had no idea how to revive an Aga.

I remembered Gwen had a similar one and rang for advice. I'd promised Mr Giles to speak to her, anyway. I pondered what he'd said. What was he sorry for?

My phone showed seventeen percent power. I'd need to talk fast.

'Hi Gwen, my phone's nearly out of battery, so need some quick advice.'

'Sure, I'm glad you're OK. Terrible weather.'

'That's precisely the problem, I'm stuck in Rooks Row. The snows too deep to get home. There's been an accident. They have airlifted Mr Giles to hospital.

'Raymond is in hospital?'

'Yes, and I have to keep his Aga going. It's almost out and there's no power. I won't have any heat if it dies.'

'I remember that Aga. It's solid fuel like mine. Open the lower door and gently turn the firebox wheel with the poker. If the box is full of ash, empty most of it out. You should see the embers glow red. Once they do, add fresh coal but slowly, so you don't suffocate it.'

'What…' she sounded strained, 'What did you say about Raymond?'

'Mr Giles, you mean? He's in a bad way, I'm afraid. A bale of hay pinned him to their barn floor. The doors were open, and he was cold; very, very cold by the time I found him.'

'Oh God no! Will he be OK?' She sounded appalled.

'I'm not certain. The paramedics seemed concerned. He gave me a message for you. In case he didn't make it,' he said.

I heard a gasp.

My battery was down to nine percent. I gabbled as fast as possible. 'He asked me to tell you he was sorry and should have waited. Got to go; my phone is nearly dead.'

I hung up, then switched it off, couldn't risk losing the last little bit of power; I might need it for another emergency. What a day. In my rush, I'd forgotten to tell Gwen that Mr Giles, who I now knew was Raymond, had said he loved her. I'd give her the full message as soon as I saw her next.

I spent an hour nursing the Aga back to life, found a tin of dog food for Hamburger, then made myself tea and poached egg on toast. We went out to check on the sheep. The snow had stopped, but a sullen grey sky glowered over the farm. More would be coming.

The silence outside was eerie, sounds muffled by the heavy fall, The only noise was the squeaking crunch of my footsteps. Piles of snow had blown in, half blocking the barn door, but I saw the sheep huddled together among the bales of hay. They'd need water, but tomorrow would do. Turning, I marvelled at the deep drifts that almost reached the upstairs windows at the rear of the house. Numbingly cold, I hurried back to the warmth of the kitchen with Hamburger struggling through the deep snow at my heels.

I couldn't spend another night in the kitchen chair and knew there were only chairs in Mr Giles' tiny sitting room. I needed to find a sofa or bed to stretch out on and explored their living room. It was a lovely space filled with polished antique oak furniture. Elegant dusty-pink curtains framed four windows looking out over the valley. At one end, a squidgy sofa faced a huge inglenook fireplace laid with logs, more set to one side. Hurrah, I wouldn't freeze then; what a pleasant room. I went into the study next. It faced east, so no light came through the drifts covering the window. Shadowy outlines of a computer on a desk and bookcase loomed before me.

I hesitated before climbing the broad staircase. I shouldn't go up uninvited, but my curiosity won out. Three double bedrooms, two modern bathrooms with marble tiles and waterfall showers, the other had an ancient restored roll-top bath and sink. Swish, like something out of a magazine. Not what I'd expected of an elderly farmer. Then I remembered, Drew's ex-wife would have designed them.

Two single bedrooms, one overlooked the front of the house and on a normal day would have had views. There were lots of drawings on a tilted specialist desk, books on architecture, and an iPhone charger, Drew's room. Without heat, the entire house felt deadly cold. I'd sleep by the fire.

As I turned to go downstairs, a light came on over my head. I heard a click as a pump sprung to life in the airing cupboard. They had repaired the power lines, excellent. Back in the study, I plugged my iPhone into the charger and switched it on. Texts from Mum, three more from Drew, a couple from Verity, Gwen and Linda.

An, *I do like to be beside the seaside* tune sounded on my phone; a reminder to check the Aga, so I rushed downstairs.

I spent the evening curled up on the sofa, tucked under a throw, watching the TV news, and moved Hamburger's basket from the kitchen to beside the fire so he could keep me company. Logs glowed in the grate whilst red-nosed journalists swaddled in thick coats and hats reported on the chaos from around Wales and the Marches. They roundly criticised the Met Office for the lack of warning. People across the country shared their problems: cars stranded, trees fallen, power lines down, pipes frozen. I enjoyed a wave of satisfaction when a Gwent farmer described his worries for his sheep, left high in the hills, with no idea if they'd survive.

In the morning, Hamburger's pink tongue licked my face and woke me. Warm and dry, it comforted me and was far nicer than Alan's beery breath. I opened the curtains to bright blue skies and a glorious view of the mountains across the shimmering lake. The snow sparked in the sunshine. It looked unspeakably beautiful.

Energised, I made breakfast. A shovel stood next to the coal store opposite the back door. Crunching through the snow, I dug a path to the barn, then lugged a full bucket of water to the sheep and poured it into a galvanised trough, hoping it wouldn't freeze. Bleating sheep quickly surrounded it.

Taking pleasure in the exercise, I excavated more snow and made a way through to the front gate. It'd help me get home all the sooner, I reasoned. Harder work than I expected. I sweated and considered throwing off my jumper when I heard a distant thrum which got louder. Selwyn, in a fake fur Russian hat with earflaps and green checked fleecy jacket, appeared on his ancient red tractor. It rumbled toward me at a stately pace.

Voice faint against the engine noise, he shouted, 'Linda told Anne, who told my missus, that you were snowed in up here. Once the council snowplough cleared the main road, she said, the wife I mean, said I had to help. Hop on, I'll take you back to your cottage.'

'Let me shut the front door,' I called. 'Will the sheep be OK in the barn?'

'I'll check on them this evening. I work for Raymond now and then to make a few bob. He'll pay me when I see him.' A shadow passed over his face. 'If he makes it, word is, he's in intensive care. Sounds like you found him in the nick of time.'

The village telegraph system meant Selwyn probably knew more about it than me.

'It's lucky that his sheep dog came to fetch me.'

'Is that how you found him? My missus wondered. No one drops by to Rooks Row. Mind, she tells me you're friendly with his son?'

I ignored the question in his tone and called Hammy to heel. I wasn't leaving him behind. Selwyn struggled to turn the tractor in the lane, while I rushed in, fed the Aga half a heavy hod of coal, and shut the door. I couldn't lock it without a key. He helped me clamber into the tiny cab, and the collie jumped up beside us.

High up, I marvelled at the views. 'Lovely isn't it?' I said.

Selwyn grunted. 'Depends how long it sticks. Damn nuisance if it stays long.'

Drew

Amy, alone in a blizzard on the mountain? I felt sick. A city girl would not understand how dangerous that could be. Dad airlifted to the hospital. I had to be there, get home. Snow fell steadily as I dialled the airline's number.

When I told the woman on the enquiry desk about my father she was sympathetic.

'We're trying to keep the runways clear, Sir. Flights will resume as soon as practical. Finland has the best equipment in the world; snow blowers, ploughs, loaders, brooms, sprayer trucks and de-icing agents. Heathrow and Gatwick's runways are another matter entirely. I can't say when they will re-open. They've canceled all flights to the UK tonight. Since you are a frequent flyer with Finnair and have family problems, I will book you on the first plane that leaves for London.'

I texted and rang Amy's number repeatedly, but each time got a leave a message notification. Her phone was off. What was happening? I couldn't bear it. Should I report her missing? What if she'd fallen in the blizzard? At four that afternoon, a text pinged through; Amy, thank God. It only said she was back in Rooks Row, but at least she was safe.

I called the hospital in Cardiff. The nurse told me that Dad was in intensive care and the doctors running tests and assessing him, and asked me to ring back in the morning.

I barely slept. Every time I closed my eyes, Amy's triumphant grin after she'd herded the sheep, followed by her forlorn expression as she told me to keep my peace offering of roses, haunted me.

I spent the morning trying to work, but couldn't concentrate. Flights left Helsinki for Chicago, New York and Berlin, but as the enquiry desk predicted, snow still paralysed the UK. A few minutes before midnight, a text informed me my flight would leave at 6.45 a.m., subject to weather conditions.

Heathrow passport control was quiet; Finnair, one of the first flights to land that morning. I was in the Range Rover and on my way home by nine-fifteen.

I rang the hospital from the car. Dad was due in theatre for an operation to straighten the femur and set his leg in an hour's time and hadn't recovered consciousness. They still wouldn't comment on how he'd be after severe hypothermia. Told me it was too soon to give a prognosis, but that brain damage remained a possibility. The news was hard to take. I'd no one to tell either; no one, apart from me, who cared about Dad.

The roads in Helsinki had been clear despite a foot of snow, but Heathrow was in chaos. Would the M4 be any better? At least the Range Rover has 4 wheel drive, I thought, passing cars abandoned on the hard shoulder. At the rate I was going, I'd have time to drive home and check on Amy before going to the hospital for five.

Conditions were dire on the A470. I crawled at 15 miles an hour behind a snow plough spewing grit to make it over the top of the Beacons. Finally, Brecon and the mountains around Talwern were in sight.

Chapter 15

Amy

By late morning, the road outside Well Cottage was passable, if treacherous, where snow had compacted. I texted Verity to see how they were and arranged for her to come over for coffee the next day. I heated a can of carrot and coriander soup and sat at the table, only for the door knocker to sound. Two yellow roses peeked through snow on the trellis around the doorway. Under them stood Gwen, in a pale blue ski jacket with a fur-lined hood, expression tense. She held a loaf of bread and passed it to me.

'Come in and warm up. Coffee or there's another can of soup?' I kissed her cheek.

'I thought you might have run out of bread,' she said and swallowed. 'Who am I trying to kid? What has happened to Raymond? How is he and what did he mean when he said sorry?'

I told her about the accident, then said, 'I forgot to tell you half of his message. I was in a rush. My phone battery...'

'Never mind. What else did he say?'

'He said he'd always loved you. That he was sorry and should have waited.'

Gwen's face crumpled as she gave a racking wail. Eventually, her sobs lessened.

'I didn't think you knew Mr Giles.'

'Oh, I know him all right. I try not to catch sight of him, ever. It hurts too much. Now, I wonder whether he felt the same.'

She cried again, but then mumbled, 'Promise you won't tell anyone and I'll explain.'

I stroked her arm as the story tumbled out.

'We were eighteen in the spring of 1985. Our families hated each other because of my great aunt and his uncle; I've told you all about that. There was another reason neither family approved. The Giles family were chapel; Calvinist Methodists, they disliked Popery. My family, the Havards, have been Catholic for centuries, as long as we've farmed here.

I knew we shouldn't meet, be friends even, but Raymond was handsome; tanned and lean from working in the fields. Quiet and intense, he seemed different from the other boys in school. Our teachers predicted he'd achieve good A level results, although his father wanted him to stay on the farm. He decided to study to become a vet. He applied, and they offered him a place in London, provided he got excellent grades, three A's. They had already accepted me for nursing in King's College. We meant to leave Talwern at the end of the summer and meet in London.

'The inevitable happened. I missed two periods and Mum noticed. It all came out. Mother was furious, more so when she discovered Raymond Giles was the father. She said I'd betrayed my family and threatened to disown me.

'I considered telling him, he'd have stuck by me, but not been able to go to college. How could students support a baby? If I had gone to Rooks Row, my parents wouldn't have spoken to me ever again. I'd no idea how his family would respond. They might have rejected me too.

They sent me to a cousin in Reading. I didn't tell Raymond why I left; just said I fancied a change.

'My family arranged for me to go into a Crusade of Rescue for Unmarried Mother's, a Catholic organisation after I'd given birth. After a long labour, I delivered a baby boy and called him Paul. The nurses sent the hospital almoner to me half an hour later. I'd barely recovered.'

She paused, rocking back and fore, grief stricken. It took a while before she continued. 'I didn't know who or what an almoner was. Turned out it was a social worker. She said it would be better for me and for the baby if a loving home with two parents adopted him. Told me Paul, being called bastard and looked after by a young unmarried woman with no future, would destroy him. Being illegitimate was something to be ashamed of then. I believed her.

'I spent six weeks in the mother and baby hostel, feeding Paul, getting to know him.' Her voice dropped to a whisper. 'Learning to love him. A moral welfare worker came and made me sign adoption papers. They took Paul away. I let them.

'I've never forgiven myself, but saw no alternative. Without a job or skills, caring for a baby seemed hopeless. My parents wouldn't allow me to come home with a child. They'd already told me I'd brought disgrace to their door. I took up my place in nursing school instead and refused to go back at Easter.

'Two months later, a letter arrived from my mother. Raymond was marrying a girl from Cardiff because she was six months pregnant. Mother crowed that the Giles family behaved true to form, betrayers, and that she'd been right. But, but she hadn't held my baby. Felt him grow inside her.'

'Three months later she wrote again, to say that Raymond had a son with that woman; Andrew. I was distraught. Somehow, a girl wouldn't have been as bad. I hated everyone here and didn't return to Talwern, not until after my father died. I couldn't forgive any of them.

'Mum admitted in her last years that it had tormented them to know they had a grandson; one they'd never meet. That our home would be sold up, not inherited, saddened them. It was all about family pride for them.'

'I'm so sorry, Gwen. That's such a sad story.' I hesitated then asked, 'Did you ever attempt to find the baby, or tell Raymond?'

'I tried to trace Paul once, twenty years ago; the Catholic church refused to give me the details of where he'd been placed or his new name. I hoped he might get in touch, once he reached eighteen and put my name on their list saying I would like contact. There was no word and it's been nearly forty years. If he knows he's adopted, he'll despise me for abandoning him; think I'm a disgrace. Now Raymond says he's always loved me. He will hate me when he finds out that I gave away my baby. Our baby.'

'I'm sure he wouldn't,' I said.

'I think of Paul every day. His brown eyes and chubby arms reaching out to me.'

The doorbell echoed round the house again. Drew stood on the doorstep, in a red scarf, Barbour jacket and flat cap.

He glared at me. 'Thank God, you're all right. Going up onto the mountain in that blizzard; you could have died. Why don't you answer your phone?' he asked. 'I've been worrying about you for two days.'

'I, I... meant to. The cold got my battery. I had no power.'

He dragged his hand through his hair, gaze exasperated, as usual.

'I want to shake you,' he said, 'and to...' Gwen appeared, red-eyed but ready to defend me. It was obvious she was upset. I was less sure what Andrew was going to do after shaking me, a part of me thrilled to imagine.

Nonplused, they stared at each other. I winced with embarrassment for them.

'Have you met? Drew, this is Gwen Havard. Gwen meet Andrew Giles.'

Gwen recovered first. 'Of course we've met, Amy. Andrew visits his father regularly. Have you seen Raymond yet? How is he?'

Drew's face clouded. He gave a cautious response. 'I've only rung. The hospital reports that Dad is semi-conscious. His femur broke in the accident, but it is the hypothermia they are concerned about. Visiting time is from five, so I'm driving there in an hour.'

He looked down and screwed his eyes up tight, forcing out, 'They are not sure if there's going to be brain damage.'

Gwen gasped in horror and swayed. Was she about to faint? I held her arm as Drew shot me a confused glance.

I said, 'Oh, Drew, I am so sorry to hear that. I'll be rooting for him. We both will.' I shook Gwen's arm. She managed a weak reply.

'We will indeed.'

He nodded. 'I'm guessing Jet is with you?'

I stared him down.

'Oh, for goodness' sake; I mean our sheepdog.'

'He is, and so you know, the only reason your father is in hospital and not dead and lying frozen and alone in your barn is because Hamburger came to fetch me.'

Outraged, I said, 'He herded your sheep down the mountain after that; so maybe, just maybe, you should be thankful and start calling him by his name.'

Drew flushed red. 'I didn't know... I.' Hammy stood beside him and licked his hand. He bent and patted the dog's head.

'I'll be getting on then. Back to Cardiff to see Dad.'

My irritation evaporated.

'How did you get here? Weren't you in Finland?'

'Caught the first flight out and followed the snow ploughs up the M4.' He shrugged. 'I was worried about you and Dad. He was in theatre having his leg set when I rang, so I came here. I needed to check you were safe. I'll drive back to the hospital as soon as I've checked the house.'

'Keep us updated,' I said, thinking, at least someone cares. Drew actually admitted he was concerned about me. 'I'll cook supper. You'll be too tired.'

Gwen grasped his hand. 'Please tell us how he's doing. Ring anytime. I'd like to visit him if… if he improves.'

Over her head, Drew's eyes telegraphed his question, 'What's going on?'

I couldn't explain after my promise to Gwen. I shrugged, shaking my head as if I'd no idea that Drew had a half brother he'd never known.

Drew

The hour long journey south to Cardiff and the hospital was easier, despite treacherous ice and slush on the road over the Beacons at Storey Arms, but at least I'd seen Amy. I thought about her as I drove; couldn't get her eyes and smile out of my head.

She was fine, glowing, in fact, thank heaven. I'd put blundered again, calling the collie Jet. Why did I do that? Stupid, stupid, I knew it'd annoy her. I would have apologised if Gwen Havard hadn't interfered. What business was it of hers?

At the hospital reception, they told me they had moved my father from intensive care to high dependency. Surely that had to be a good sign? But there again, perhaps they needed the bed for someone sicker or, or younger. My stomach knotted back up as I walked into the ward. The smell of antiseptic and the bleeping of machines took me back to the time after Dad had his stroke. He was at the far end, wired to a heart monitor with drips in both arms, leg in plaster and elevated. He looked old and frail, half the man he'd been three years ago.

'Dad, it's me. It's Drew. Whatever happened?'

He groaned and opened his eyes. Slurring, he said, 'All I remember was the dog pulling at me. He brought that niece of Jen's. I… we had a good chat. Discussed the past.'

He paused, Dad's a man of few words. I didn't expect what came next.

'We talked about the mistakes I've made. Your mother… and not following your heart. Don't do the same as me, Andrew, and follow a miserable path to loneliness. You may have married the wrong woman the first time around, but that doesn't mean you are destined to be alone. For heavens sake, don't make the mess of your life I've made of mine. You're the only decent thing I've ever done.'

He closed his eyes, a glimmer of moisture under the lids.

'Dad, you mustn't say that. You've worked hard, accomplished so much with the farm. There's cash in the bank and you gave me a lovely home.'

My voice trailed off as it hit me. I was a success, my architecture practice thrived, work filled every hour and there was indeed plenty of money in the bank. With no one to share it with, it felt empty, lonely and meaningless.

Dad didn't respond. I wasn't sure if he was asleep or unconscious so squeezed his hand. There was no response. The heart monitor still beeped regularly. An

146

Asian doctor wearing pale green scrubs, stethoscope slung around her neck, walked down the ward towards me.

'Did I see your father talking to you?'

I nodded.

'And he made sense?'

'Yes,' I sighed, 'a lot of sense.'

'That's good. We were worried he might have brain damage; hopefully not. He should recover reasonably quickly from the hypothermia. I imagine we'll transfer him to the orthopaedic ward in the next few hours, as long as everything stays stable.'

'Is he asleep or unconscious?'

The doctor looked at his chart, took Dad's pulse, and smiled. 'Asleep. They'll have given him powerful pain relief while they set the leg. He'll be drowsy for hours. I can't give any guarantees, but he should be fine. He'll need physio once he's weight bearing, especially given the history of stroke. You may have to arrange carers for a few while. The social work team will discuss that after they have assessed him.

My heart sank. It was impossible to imagine my impatient, irascible father agreeing to carers. I'd have to take compassionate leave and work from Talwern. Hand over the day to day Finnish project to one of the youngsters in the team. They'd relish it. Sally kept hinting I should allow the associates to do more. "Supervise not monopolise," she'd suggested months ago.

I thanked the doctor, patted Dad's hand, and at the last minute bent to kiss his forehead. I hadn't kissed my father since I was a tiny child. As I did so, his hand caught mine.

'Don't follow in my footsteps, boy. Grab your chances while you can,' came a hoarse whisper.

I left the warmth of the ward to be hit by freezing winds and snow flurries as I made for the car park. There was only one place I longed to be and if I didn't want to become ensnared by the weather, I had to leave, and quickly.

Amy

Gwen pulled on furry topped snow boots to leave ten minutes after Drew went.

'I'll ring to let you know how Raymond is, the second Drew gets back and say you want to visit his father as soon as possible. How will I explain? Does he realise you were once friends?'

'He might. Memories run long in the countryside. Be vague, Raymond may have forgotten what he said if he was in a bad way.' Her face was tormented and drawn, eyes distant. 'If Raymond's brain damaged, I'll never know what he meant. Never be able to explain why I left.'

She put on her coat and strode out to her car. Snow flakes filled the sky once again. I closed the door and thought of Drew driving from the hospital in this terrible weather. He might stay at his mother's in Cardiff. I half hoped he would; he'd be safe then. I had time to prepare, but not much fresh food left: onions, a butternut squash and a few peppers. A veggie stew was the best I could manage. I remembered an ancient shrink-wrapped beef steak in the bottom of Jen's freezer among all the icy gubbins. I put it in lukewarm water to defrost and set a bottle of Merlot next to the log burner.

I checked my mobile in a couple of hours. Two texts; one from Drew twenty-five minutes earlier, saying he was on his way and would take me up on my offer of supper. A mixture of pleasure and anxiety hit me. It was an awful night to travel, but he was coming. Would he be OK? What if he had an accident? I took a look at Google maps. It showed delays for almost the entire journey.

Three quarters of an hour later, snow scrunched outside as a car pulled up, Drew. I rushed to the door and flung it open. There he was, stamping his feet with the cold, in his green waxed jacket, gloves and scarf. I was stumped, unsure how to greet him after the row the last time we met. He hesitated too, as we gazed at each other. Awkward; neither of us knowing whether to hug, or do the kiss, kiss on the cheeks thing? Should I shake his hand, hug him in sympathy? Do something; anything, I thought.

He leant forward, as I stood back to let him in. He sort of tumbled into me and grabbed my shoulders to steady himself. His scarf met my mouth as I supported him. He may have been trying to kiss my cheek, but he missed. We straightened up as Hamburger leapt between us, licking at Drew's hands as he pulled off his gloves.

'Come in out of the cold. How's your dad? Must have been a terrible journey? Take the sofa by the fire.

Hammy sit,' I gabbled and rushed to put on another log, avoiding eye contact. Complexion grey, Drew appeared totally exhausted.

'Dad talked sense, thank goodness. Just a couple of sentences. He was drowsy because of the painkillers and mostly slept, but I'm glad to say that they don't think there's brain damage.'

'That's great news.'

Drew dragged a hand over his forehead. 'Mmm, Dad looked awful. Wired up to all sorts of machines, with his leg in plaster. I barely recognised him. He mentioned you; said you'd had a chat and talked about the past.'

'We did. I'll tell you about it over supper. You must be starving. Pour yourself some wine and I'll fetch in the food.'

'I finally get my glass of wine?' He raised an eyebrow at the sight of his steak and my butternut stew. 'You didn't have to cook meat for me. I'd have eaten vegetarian, the same as you.'

'It's fine. I make meat dishes at home for my parents and did for my ex, he insisted. Never mind that. Eat up while I explain about your father and Gwen Havard. Did you know they were childhood sweethearts?'

'I remember a few comments when she came back to Talwern, now you mention it.'

'He was Gwen's first love, but their parents didn't approve of the match.'

'My grandparents didn't approve of much from what I recollect. Made my mother's life a misery; that was part of why my parents split up.'

'Gwen and your dad meant to meet in London after he took his place in veterinary school.'

'Dad wanted to be a vet? Are you sure? I thought he'd always intended to farm. He's never said he planned to go to college.'

'I'm certain. Gwen told me all about it. She was going to complete her nurse training whilst he studied. She, um, left and while she was away, your father met your mother.'

'That explains a lot. Why Dad encouraged me to pursue my dream of becoming an architect. He reassured me, said not to fret about the farm. I've always known my parents had to marry because Mum was pregnant. They had me five months after the wedding. With me on the way, I guess university wasn't possible.' Drew said. 'But I've never seen him speak to Gwen Havard, not in the two years she's been back. What has changed? Why is she so keen to visit him?'

'That chat you mentioned? Your father thought he was going to die and asked me to tell Gwen he'd never stopped loving her. That he was sorry for not waiting.'

'Goodness, and she's sorry too?' he asked.

'That's right. She is waiting for me to get in touch, to update her how he is. In fact, I should do that. Sit by the fire while I call her. I'll bring pudding through after I've spoken to her.'

On the phone, I filled Gwen in, told her Raymond was seriously ill but didn't appear to have any brain damage. I offered to ask Drew to take her to the hospital next day. Then I cleared up the kitchen and

151

carried through two bowls of Aunt Jen's bottled prunes in brandy with ice-cream.

Head lolling to one side, Drew was fast asleep the sofa, with Hamburger curled beside him. No wonder, he was worn out after all the travelling that day. I put a cushion on his shoulder, placed a knitted throw over him, and crept up to bed. We'd talk in the morning.

Thirty minutes later, the knocker sounded through the cottage. Hamburger barked and growled in response. Who on earth could it be at this time of night? I struggled into my dressing gown and slippers and made my way down, to overhear Drew arguing with Simon Evans on the doorstep.

Their voices echoed up the stairs.

'What do you want? It's late,' asked Drew.

'I… what are you doing here, at, at my girlfriend's this time of night?' Simon asked.

Outraged I yelled, 'I've never been your girlfriend, Simon Evans. Haven't set eyes on you for weeks.'

Drew's voice was steady. 'I'm here because Amy's invited me, unlike you. It's late to turn up, especially in that state. Your face is a mess.'

What state, I wondered? I pushed past Andrew into the doorway.

Simon's nose trickled blood onto his chin. One eye puffed, swollen and purple, he had a cut to his cheek.

'What's happened? Have you crashed your bike?'

Drew folded his arms. 'Someone's given him a pasting that's what's happened; most of us in the village can guess who.'

What, who…? I asked.

Simon glared at Drew, who stood solid and unmoving beside me.

'Like I said, it's late and you're not welcome. I suggest you leave, go home and clean up,' said Drew.

Simon turned to hobble down the path to his bike

I was relieved he was with me. Simon might easily have barged in if I'd been alone. I didn't trust him and would have been scared to let him sleep on the sofa; afraid he'd come up to my room. I'd not given a second's thought to allowing Drew to sleep downstairs overnight. Chalk and cheese those two.

'You've never been his girlfriend?' asked Drew. He sounded surprised.

'No, we went on a couple of double dates with Ben and Verity; they were rubbish. He was a self-obsessed creep. Didn't give him my number. Why he turned up here tonight, I can't imagine.' I shrugged. 'Why ever did you think I was going out with him?'

Drew looked embarrassed. 'I saw you in the pub, and he had his arm around you. I thought…' His voice trailed off.

'What did you mean, when you said most people will know who hit him?' I asked.

Drew sighed. 'It's not for me to tell you. I'll be getting on back to Rooks Row. People will talk if they see my car outside overnight. You should have woken me. I will telephone Gwen in the morning and if the hospital gives the go-ahead, we'll visit Dad together. Thanks for supper. Speak tomorrow.'

He hesitated, turned back and pulled me towards him. I looked into his eyes as he bent and our lips met. My heart pounded and I closed my eyes.

153

Gently pushing me away, he said, 'I'd better leave now,' as our bodies separated. He went, Hammy following close at his heels.

My head spun as I shut the door and went back to bed. He'd thought I was dating Simon. Was that why he was so cautious? Drew was right about village gossip. It wasn't Bristol. If he'd stayed, it would have gone round the village in a flash. He said most people would know who'd hit Simon. I'd a nasty suspicion as to why that was. Then I remembered his kiss and smiled.

Chapter 16

Amy

At eleven the next morning, I put on the kettle and pulled out a box of mince pies. Verity would enjoy them as a Christmas treat. The phone rang at 11.15.

Her voice sounded strained and hoarse. 'Hi Amy, I can't come. Ben's gone. There's no one to look after the children while I'm out.'

'What do you mean, "gone"? What's happened?'

The crying got louder.

'I'm on my way,' I said, then pushed on my walking boots, grabbed the mince pies and tramped through the snow down the road to The Oaks. I'd guessed who'd walloped Simon, and why everyone in the village knew.

Verity opened the door, face swollen from tears, hair dishevelled.

'Oh Amy, what have I done?' she wailed.

'Where are the kids?'

'Upstairs, watching DVDs.'

I hugged her. 'Simon?'

Her shoulders dropped. 'Simon.'

'Come on, let's make a cup of tea. You can tell me about it.'

She started slowly, said, 'It was hard moving to Talwern, making new friends. In London, there were people from my old life, from college. People who remembered how I used to be. I could talk about music to him. He seemed to really hear me, to like me was interested; at first.

'There is no one round here who cares about music. The other mums are lovely but have no genuine interest or knowledge. With Ben working away two or three days a week, it was so lonely. Simon is a musician and seemed the only person who loved music the way I did. Ben didn't understand the buzz performing gives. Simon could. One thing led to another.' Her voice trailed off. She looked down at the floor, wouldn't meet my eye.

I nodded, 'Ben didn't guess? He liked Simon. You complained about it.'

'That was the worst part, that and the guilt. After four months, I came to my senses and wanted the affair to stop and told Simon so. By then, he'd convinced Ben they were best mates. Ben expected to spend most of our free time with him. Ben was pleased when Simon appeared interested in you.'

I gasped. 'Were you and he still…? When Simon asked me out?'

She nodded miserably. 'Yes, I kept trying to finish it, but he'd threaten to tell Ben. I hated him and the deception by the end.'

'So what happened last night?'

Ben came back. I was so relieved to see him and that he was OK after driving through the blizzards to get home to look after us. We… we made up. He's been criticising me, saying that I'm drinking too much for months; but these last couple of days were perfect. I was living a lie. Simon's threats to tell Ben hung over me. I told Ben, grovelled, said I'd been a fool.

156

'What did he say?' I asked.

'After we talked, he went quiet. Chopped a pile of wood for the stove in the garden. Took the children sledging. Couldn't look me in the face, he asked for time.

'Last night Simon turned up. Ben opened the door to him and accused him of trying to break up our marriage. Simon was his usual self and tried to bluff his way out. Implied it was all in my imagination. They got into a fight and Ben sent him packing, but screamed and ranted afterwards. He told me I'd made him appear an idiot, having an affair with a man he believed to be his best friend. Ben left after midnight in a fury. I texted his mother this morning, who told me he was safe, thank heaven.'

She gripped my arm and said, 'Ben was so angry. The thought of him driving so late at night, in such dreadful conditions, in that mood. It terrified me. My children would be fatherless if he'd crashed. Life without him is unthinkable.'

I went for it. 'Simon is a scumbag, you know. He came round to my place after the fight. He had the cheek to think I'd take him in. Drew was there and sent him packing.'

'I realised that months ago, but he'd trapped me. He has such a reputation. At first I tried to warn you off, but jealousy overtook me. I was so confused. When you turned him down, Simon complained and told me to stop meeting you. He wanted to control what I did and who I saw. I'm so messed up. Say, do you fancy a drink?'

'Verity, it's lunchtime. The children are home.'

She nodded, face desolate. 'You're right, but however will I manage without Ben?'

I trudged back to Well Cottage, unsure what to think. Had she used me as camouflage? She'd said Simon appeared interested in me. Appeared. Had it all been a ruse?

Drew

I whistled as I drove to Gwen's next morning. Amy had made it clear she and Simon weren't dating; what's more, they never had been. A weight lifted from my chest, it had been my imagination.

I pulled up at Gwen's. By the time I'd opened the car door, she'd locked her front door and was hurrying towards me. I recognised her scent as she got into the passenger seat, Chanel Number 5.

She looked smart in a wool jacket, and navy trousers, but her eyes betrayed strain. At least there were no tears today. We smiled at each other, polite. Whatever would I talk to this woman about for the hour-long journey to the hospital?

'The roads should be cleared of snow by now.'

She nodded her agreement. I tried again, 'So you and Dad. You were friends in school?'

'Yes, good friends.'

'What was he like back then? He's never talked about his school days. Changed the topic if I asked. I don't even know what O and A Levels he studied.'

She smiled then. 'Raymond excelled at everything; English, sciences, sport. The only subjects he disliked were art and R. E. He came top of the class, all A's and B's.'

'That's interesting. I guessed I inherited my enjoyment of art from Mum. I remember him being astonished when I showed ability and could draw well. What is R. E.?'

'Religious Education, it was compulsory back then. We had to take two lessons a week,' she said. 'Raymond complained that he spent long enough in chapel every Sunday, without having to learn it in school.'

I nodded. 'When I was little, it annoyed my grandparents that he refused to take me to the Sunday service. That we spent the day out on the hills or doing jobs around the farm. Dad said since he couldn't see as much of me as he'd like, that he'd spend time with me, not waste it by sitting all morning being preached at in their precious chapel.'

It surprised me how sad telling her about that made me feel. I'd buried those feelings for years.

'It must have been tough, having divorced parents?' she asked.

'Yes, back then divorce was less common and, and, and,' I paused, trying to find the words to explain. 'I felt guilty all the time; missing Dad and wanting to be in Talwern when I was at home in Cardiff. Then, in Talwern I missed Mum and my brother and sister. I spent my childhood worrying about what was happening in the place I wasn't.'

'Your mother remarried?'

'She did, three years later, when I was seven. My step-father is a lovely man. He'd a son of his own and

159

they had my little sister together a couple of years later. I'm not complaining. I had a happy childhood, and was lucky compared to many. Mum and both my fathers supported everything I did. But Dad, Raymond I mean, was always sad and lonely. I never worked out why. These last two years, it's been worse.'

'In what way?'

'Dad recovered from the stroke, but a year afterwards, he became depressed and couldn't be bothered with anything much. He refused to be seen in public, and wouldn't go to the pub or the cattle market at all. Kept saying he was an embarrassment, was obsessed by the thought of it.'

'That would have been just after I came home to Talwern,' Gwen said.

'I guess so. Amy says he's improved on the medication, but I do not know how he'll be when you visit. Don't expect too much.'

I glanced sideways. She wiped her face with a tissue; was she crying again?

'I won't, but I need to see him. We were very close, and although it was years ago, sometimes it seems like yesterday. I have to tell him I'm sorry for everything that happened.'

She lapsed into a silence I didn't feel I could disturb, or ask why she was sorry. I hoped Dad would agree to see her. He'd been irritable and unpredictable recently. I wouldn't put it past him to refuse.

At the hospital reception desk, they told us they had moved him to the orthopaedic ward up on the 6th floor. I let out a breath. He was off high dependency. It had to be a progress.

We walked into the unit and a nurse directed us to a single room at the far end of the ward. Through the blind I saw Dad, leg elevated, thin, grey hair awry. He looked old, far older than Gwen. I couldn't believe this woman with fashionably cut hair and clothes was the same age as my father.

When we entered, he didn't open his eyes. Was he asleep?

'Hi Dad, it's Drew. How are you this afternoon?'

He didn't move or look up.

He said, 'All right, the leg hurts. You shouldn't have bothered coming. It's too far. Go to your mother's for an hour instead. Don't waste your time with me.'

Would he be rude to Gwen? I wondered. Hurt her feelings and refuse to speak? I wished I'd checked.

'Dad, I've brought someone with me. Gwen, Gwen Havard.'

Chapter 17

Drew

I hesitated before clicking the left indicator to turn down the lane to the farm. Should I drop in to Amy's? The dog was with her. I'd say I'd called to collect him as an excuse. In truth, I longed to see her. She'd like to know what happened in the hospital between Gwen and Dad. It'd be good to discuss it, and her cottage was cosy, not empty and silent like Rooks Row.

I trod on the brake and walked up the path but saw her back door stood open and she was by her car. Hamburger, as I had to call him from now on, gambolled in the snow, chasing his tail nearby. He raced to me, barked, then charged back towards Amy, scattering snow all over her. She knelt on a red, flowery cushion beside her little Honda, struggling to attach what looked like grey nylon shower caps to her tyres.

'Whatever are you doing?'

'Trying to put snow socks on my car. They've torn my nails to bits.'

She held out a yellow bag, which did indeed have Tyre Snow Socks written on the front. She looked so lovely kneeling there, an anxious frown on her face that I longed to take her into my arms.

'I hate driving in snow, and these are supposed to stop your car skidding.'

We looked dubiously at the material, it looked like tent sheeting.

'Do you have to get to work? It's late to set out.'

'No, everyone's been told stay at home until it's safe to travel. I'm out of food. No veg, milk or bread. Every supermarket's delivery slots are fully booked. I've got to go into Brecon, this afternoon.'

'I don't fancy your chances getting up the hill with those. They'll rip to shreds when you get onto the tarmac. Downhill will be worse. You might skid. Let me take you in the 4x4, it's the least I can do. I'll buy myself fresh food, while I'm there.'

The relief on her face said enough; she didn't want to drive in the snow at all.

'That'd be great, as long as you are sure?'

'Would you mind if we went to Abergavenny? I should pop in to my place. It's been empty throughout this cold spell. I'd like to check for burst pipes and that the central heating is working.'

'Of course, if I can buy bread and milk and maybe some tofu, I don't care where we go.'

Maybe leave the dog here? It's not worth taking him, he can't come into a supermarket.

Amy hoisted herself up into the front seat. It felt nice to have her sitting beside me.

I took my chance and apologised again. 'I'm sorry about what I said. It was totally out of order. I'd had a terrible week at work. There was a motorbike in the village and after my trips abroad, I was...was,' I grappled for the words, then came clean, 'jealous and hated it.'

She rested her hand on my arm briefly. 'OK, apology accepted. Really accepted. We all say things we don't mean sometimes.'

163

'So what happened at the hospital?' she asked, changing the subject.

'It was peculiar. When I told Dad Gwen Havard was with me, his eyes flew open. He tried to lever himself upright and ran his fingers through his hair to tidy it. He said, "You came?" and sounded astonished. Gwen didn't say anything, just walked over to the bed and took his hand.

'Dad told me to pop to the hospital shop and buy him orange squash, and come back in half an hour. It was an order, not a suggestion. When I returned, Gwen sat on a chair beside him. They were still holding hands.

'Dad looked happier than I've seen him these last three years; perhaps longer. He told me to drive Gwen back to visit tomorrow, but then leave them. Said he and Gwen had a lot to catch up on.'

'Goodness, they've made up, after what, forty years, since leaving school? I'm so pleased. I'll ring Gwen tonight and try to find out anymore.'

We'd reached the Aber Valley road. I turned the wheel and the car inched its way through deep snow.

'Sorry, I hadn't expected conditions to be so much worse here. This side of the mountains gets more snow when the wind blows from the east. It's not far, we'll be fine.'

I was surprised by Amy's cool reaction to my house. It has won awards, most people tell me it's fabulous. Amy complimented it, but it was clear that she prefers the farm. Likes it because it was old, and has a history. I gazed around at the hard shiny surfaces of Aber House and understood. When Amy said she thought Rooks Row was perfect, a lump rose in my throat. She was what was perfect.

Amy

It was such a relief when Drew offered to drive me to the shops, I nearly kissed him. I didn't, of course. That would take neighbourliness too far. Driving in snow is yet another thing that terrifies me, along with dogs, and water sports. I hate to appear girly and pathetic, when that's not the person I am at all. When Drew said he'd like to check on his house I was delighted. Who wouldn't want to see someone's home? Tells you a lot about them, Gran always says.

It felt cosy in the car, with wonderful views over the hedges. I wasn't used to sitting so high up. My little Honda is low to the ground, unlike his Range Rover. Drew told me about Gwen and his father. I took the opportunity and asked about Simon and Verity.

'Drew, when you said last night that you had to get home, otherwise people would talk?'

'Yes,' he replied, voice cautious.

'Did you mean to imply that people talked about Simon? Simon and Verity?'

'Suppose so. I guessed you didn't know they were having an affair and have wondered whether they used you as a smoke-screen, to hide what was going on from her husband. Who seems a nice bloke, by the way?'

'I'm sure Verity wouldn't even have thought that. She says she wanted to end it, but Simon threatened to tell Ben.'

'Maybe. He's certainly more than capable of that.'

'Vee kept warning me about him, said he was a womaniser. It can't have all been pretence, surely. She's my friend.'

Drew nodded, noncommittal.

Road conditions worsened after the car turned and crunched through deeper snow up a winding country lane. Finally, he stopped, opened a gate and drove up a short drive towards a square glass and wooden building on metal stilts, then pressed a button behind the sun visor and a double garage door slid up silently.

'I'll be ten minutes. Do you want to come up? We can grab a coffee, as long as you don't mind it without milk?'

I followed him up an open tread oak staircase into an amazing space. Like on the TV, a truly amazing space. A glass wall looked out over the mountains, with a narrow glass floor beneath the wall, which revealed a stream bubbling its way downhill over silvery icicles under the house. It felt magical, if disconcerting. I nearly giggled, thinking I'd need to visit the toilet all the time if I lived there.

The room was minimalist with limestone tiles and reclaimed oak beams. A vast sofa, styled with Welsh tweed throws and sheepskins was overhung by a curved standard lamp, perfectly positioned to take in the views. To one side, stood a freestanding log burner and a range of grey kitchen units filled the rear wall. Flat, glossy, perfect; with an integrated oven, microwave and, naturally, I realised, watching Drew put a capsule into a slot, a state of the art coffee-maker.

'Goodness, this place is like something out of a magazine, sleek and minimal. It's well, wow.'

Drew watched my response.

'That's what everyone says. It has featured in several glossy mags as it happens. My ex-wife designed the interior decor. I designed the basics, made sure that the balcony and glass structures worked. I bought the plot years back, before I met her.'

He paused, and rubbed his mouth. 'I've got to check the boiler and the wood chip hod. I'll be two ticks.'

As he went out, I thought it was no wonder he'd left Hammy at home. Dog hair on this floor? How would anyone dare live in this perfect space? Elegant and clinical, but not exactly a home, more of a film set.

I picked up my espresso, half expecting George Clooney to appear at the doorway. I tried to put in a second capsule in, ready for Drew, but was flummoxed by the machine.

Drew returned. 'Everything seems in order. I haven't spent much time here since Dad's stroke. I've thought of selling or renting the place out as an Air BNB. But, I put such a lot of effort into building it, I can't let go. His shoulders sagged, 'The farm seemed more like home after Steph left.'

'Rooks Row is lovely. The rooms are homely and the views are wonderful. I love that you can touch the past, imagine so many generations living there. It's perfect. Not, not that here isn't great as well,' I added lamely. Drew's an architect, he's designed this house.

For heaven's sake, you've put your foot in it, I thought. How could I dig myself out of this faux pas?

'It is tough letting go. I hated selling my flat after Alan left me. It felt like I'd failed at everything when we packed up and the removers came.'

He stared at me thoughtfully. 'Yes, but I guess it's time to let go, for us both. Don't you?'

I couldn't hold his gaze. 'We should get going or the shops will close. They won't keep staff late in this weather.'

'Waitrose or Morrisons?' he asked.

'Morrisons, the prices in Waitrose are shocking.'

'A girl after my father's heart, he uses exactly those words. Come on then, let's find you your canary food.'

'Huh, healthy and tasty; nothing wrong with vegetarian supplies.'

'I'm a farmer, we've bred beef cattle for generations. I'm not sure can I agree.' His eyes twinkled as he replied. He was teasing me.

Morrison's shelves had been emptied, bare of both fresh meat and veg. Drew found two frozen baguettes and dried milk. The shelves still held lots of tofu, jars of antipasti, falafel mix and noodles. I gloated, saying, 'See, vegetarians can survive adversity, not like you carnivores.'

I filled my shopping trolley, knowing that I'd not get another chance until it thawed.

'People in the country rush to the shops as soon as they get a weather warning. I'm not surprised the shop's empty. Dad will have plenty of stores in,' Drew said.

168

I blushed, as I realised he hadn't needed to go to the shops at all; he was just being thoughtful. Shopping together was nice; it felt comfortable. In the dog food section, Drew bought two multipacks of tinned meat. I insisted on adding dog biscuits and chews to the trolley.

'I've been reading up. Dogs need roughage, and chews to keep their teeth clean, as well as the occasional treat.' I looked at him sideways and added, 'You were right about chocolate biscuits, back in the autumn, when you ah, told me off. They're not great treats for dogs.'

He threw up his hands in mock amazement. 'Did I hear you say I was right, Dr Stuart? That's a first.' I poked an elbow into his ribs and as he fought me off, I felt tingles down my spine at his touch. He pulled me towards him and held my waist on the way back to the car.

'You'll be suggesting a trip to McDonald's next,' he said with a grin.

'Do you think it would be open? Hammy deserves a treat after all he did for your father. I planned to buy one for him next time I drive back from Bristol. Come to that, I wouldn't mind a veggie burger myself. I'm hungry.'

Drew gave a pantomime groan. 'We'll check on the way home. I'll pay, but only because it's a cheap date.'

Back at Well Cottage he carried in my groceries, then fetched more wood for the log burner from the wood store.

We looked at each other. I couldn't offer to cook; he'd devoured an entire Big Mac quarter pounder and

169

chips, but I didn't want him to leave and was certain he didn't want to go.

'Thanks for the lift and carrying everything. I've a bottle of wine chilling, or there's beer?' I asked.

'That'd be lovely, just like you,' he said, and pulled me into his arms. As I melted into his embrace, it felt like coming home. We tumbled onto the sofa, unable to stop kissing.

At eleven, Drew released me and said, 'I'd best get back to feed the Aga. I'll sort out the sheep tomorrow morning and pop in before driving Gwen to visit Dad. Come on, Hammy, let's go.'

I nodded, taking things slowly felt the right thing to do. Everything was different with Drew. He confused me and comforted me all at once.

Drew

At Rooks Row I found a white car with a Hertz sticker on its windscreen parked in the yard. Who on earth?

Steph sat on the sofa beside the inglenook. The fire's glow reflected in a glass of red, which she picked up as I entered the room. Elegant, perfectly manicure fingers cupped the wine. Her low cut silk blouse revealed a tasteful sliver of red satin underwear; a set piece. She'd arranged herself to please. Why?

'Drew, darling. Lovely to see you.'

She patted the sofa beside to her.

Ignoring the gesture, I stood in front of the fire and crossed my arms. 'Stephanie, what the hell are you doing here? How did you get into the house?'

She shrugged. 'The key's under the usual stone. I let myself in.'

'But why are you here?'

Her face expressed hurt, her mouth flattened pathetically. 'I'm back in the UK for a while. Why shouldn't I drop in on my favourite man?'

'Because we're divorced, for Christ's sake.'

'Ah, well, we all make mistakes.' A laugh tinkled as she stood, smoothed her hair, then looked up through long eyelashes; ones that were actually extensions. 'You are late, though. Been to the pub with your farming friends?'

She stepped towards me and tweaked my collar straight. Something she'd often done when we'd first met. I'd seen her do it to other men. It gave them a chance to smell her perfume, look down her cleavage. It had overwhelmed me on early dates. Now I was immune.

'Where I've been is no concern of yours. We divorced over a year ago. I'd like you to leave.'

'What, at this time of night, and in this weather? You can't be serious. I couldn't possibly drive, the roads are too dangerous.' Her face set into the sulky pout I recognised. It was an argument I was unlikely to win. Short of carrying her to the car and locking the front door behind her, I'd get nowhere. Besides, there was a Met Office yellow warning of ice. The police had asked everyone to stay at home unless absolutely necessary.

'OK, you can sleep in the spare room and leave first thing. Goodnight.'

In bed, I reflected that she hadn't asked about Dad. Did she even wonder where he was?

Next morning I woke at seven to the smell of frying bacon. Steph never cooked for breakfast. She liked me to bring tea and one slice of toast to her in bed.

I went into the kitchen. She smiled pleasantly and said, 'There you are. Breakfast is ready. I'll brew us fresh coffee.'

'Steph, finish your cereal and leave. I'll make my own breakfast, as I have for over two years.'

'I have to wait for conditions to improve.'

I clenched my teeth, resisting the urge to shout. 'They've gritted the roads. You got here OK. You'll get back.'

I heard scratching at the door.

'I put the dog out into the yard. You know how unhygienic it is to have them in a room where you cook. I kept telling your father that. Where is he, by the way?' she asked.

I couldn't believe the woman. My head buzzed with fury. It was well below freezing; to send Hamburger outside was cruel beyond belief, and to ask so casually about Dad, her father-in-law for five years. The man who'd gritted his teeth and let her get the builders in and reshape his home, when he liked it as it was.

The front doorbell sounded. Who was that?

I opened the door to find Amy with a McDonald's box in hand and a bright smile on her face. Her cheeks and the tip of her nose glowed pink in the cold.

'We forgot to give Hammy his burger....' Her voice trailed off.

Stephanie stood beside me in the doorway and laughed in the same tinkling tone she had yesterday. A fake laugh, one to confound. She put her hand on my arm. 'And who is this, Drew? I don't remember many neighbours calling?' she asked.

Amy stiffened. It was eight in the morning and obvious that Steph had stayed the night. What must she think?

Hammy slunk around the corner towards us. He looked cold and ran to Amy for reassurance.

'Amy, meet my ex-wife. She called in unexpectedly last night. It was too icy for her to drive back to London. She is about to leave.'

Stephanie had tensed. 'Yes, I should get on. Lovely to catch up, Drew. The bed was soo comfortable,' she purred, then stroked my back. I'd a suspicion she'd winked at Amy as she mentioned bed. That sort of innuendo was so like her.

Amy's eyes widened and hurt and confusion filled them. She hurried down the path. The collie followed, sniffing at the red box in her hand.

What the hell was going on with Stephanie? Why was she in Talwern and not the US? No wonder she'd upset Amy. Damn her. I'd have to explain to Amy, the second Steph left.

Steph turned. 'Whoever was that strange girl in the dreadful coat, Drew? And while we are talking about

173

clothes, whatever are you wearing? What's with the worn check flannel shirt and cords? Grandad chic makes you seem ancient. Where's your Hugo Boss kit? You need to dress the part of a successful architect, not a stuffy middle-aged farmer.'

'Steph get out. Just go. You've tried my patience long enough. I'm due to visit my father. He's in hospital; not that you've asked.' As Steph left, I remembered how she'd got in.

'I'll have the key back, please.'

'Drew are you sure? I may need it next time. Be easier if I keep it, surely?'

'There's not going to be a next time. Dad wouldn't want you here uninvited'

She rummaged in her outsize bag and finally came up with the key, then gazed up into my eyes and licked her lips. 'Are you sure you don't want to see me again? We could go back inside. Try again?' She'd lowered her voice. It sounded husky and was followed by that tinkling laugh.

What was she up to?

'I'm certain.' On impulse I added, 'By the way don't try the same trick in Aber House. I changed the alarm code. Didn't like that it was your birthday.'

Her expression changed, hardened, so did her voice. 'As if,' she said.

I thought huh, I'm pretty sure that was the plan. Didn't the woman have anywhere else to go? I handed over the designer handbag and stood blocking the hallway. She had no option but return to the rental car.

I watched her drive away with relief. Had we ever actually liked each other? I didn't think so; I'd lusted after her, and she'd viewed me as another project, something to improve. Not really, neither of us liked each other.

As usual, her criticism hit a nerve. I'd worn comfortable clothes at home in Talwern for the last couple of years. I fitted in better in the pub and the farm supplies shop. My trendy London clothes stayed in my wardrobe in the Chiswick flat.

I glanced into the hall mirror; a forty-year-old man with salt and pepper hair stared back at me. That was how I looked to Amy. Young and pretty, men of her age dressed like Simon Evans, not Selwyn. I needed to smarten my Talwern appearance and up my game.

Chapter 18

Amy

I went to bed with a warm glow in my stomach. It had been such a lovely day and night. When Drew kissed me, it felt right. We'd spent three hours on the sofa, holding hands, kissing, nuzzling, caressing, until I was breathless with desire. I grappled with how to ask if he wanted to stay. His car was outside, and that he'd insist on driving it back to the farm. How could I suggest he return on foot without sounding sex starved? I wasn't sure what to do for the best.

Drew finally let me go and left. I decided against asking him to stay and to take things slowly for a change, not rush in. Somehow I knew I needn't worry. I was certain he'd call in tomorrow.

Early the next morning, my phone buzzed. It was Gwen.

'Hi, Amy. Lovely day. How are you?'

'It is, but never mind me. What happened in the hospital yesterday?'

Her voice sounded dreamy. 'Raymond was improving. It was as if the years fell away. All the anger.'

'And?'

'We held hands.'

She sounded giddy, delighted.

'We talked about the nurses, Drew.' She coughed, 'You.'

A note of anxiety crept into her voice. 'I haven't told him about the baby, about Paul. He's bound to ask why I didn't keep in touch. Amy, what if he hates me?'

'Of course he won't.'

'I've decided not to put it off. It will get harder to say the words if I do. I'm going to tell him about Paul today. You didn't think less of me. Perhaps Raymond will be the same.'

'I've got to know him this last month. He's kind, Gwen. It will be OK.'

'I hope you're right. I'd better get ready now. Drew will pick me up in a couple of hours.'

'Sure, speak soon.' I laughed. How could getting dressed take two hours? Gwen was acting like the schoolgirl she'd been when they'd split up.

Clearing up in the front room, I found the burger in its box. We'd forgotten about it when we got back. There'd been more pressing matters.

Hammy wouldn't care if it was cold. It was a bright morning, a walk would do me good. I'd call in to Rooks Row before Drew left for the hospital.

The snow melted as the sun warmed the land, but the lane to Rooks Row remained icy and treacherous underfoot. In the farmyard there was a white car parked, one I'd never seen before. It was early for visitors. Hammy ran towards me from the barn, tail down. Strange, I usually found him curled in his basket by the Aga first thing.

Drew opened the front door. I held out the burger box in explanation, but a slim, dark-haired woman appeared behind him. Immaculately made up, in an expensive cream cable knit teamed with long, leather boots over jeans; she looked like a model. My grubby gardening clothes and Jen's borrowed old anorak made me embarrassed in comparison. The woman grasped Drew's arm possessively, then laughed at me.

No wonder he was keen to get home last night if this woman was waiting. But why did he kiss me? Was he a player like all the rest?

Drew looked embarrassed, then introduced her as his ex, Stephanie. But do ex's stay over? Alan certainly didn't.

Then the woman implied they'd slept together, said the bed was comfortable. It was clear what she meant by her laughter and a wink. She was warning me off. There was no need. I'd never stand a chance against a woman that looked like that.

I had to get away and rushed from the door only to slip, almost falling on black ice by the gate. My cheeks burnt red with embarrassment and fury. How could I have got it so wrong? Why did Drew toy with me last night?

I'd found yet another bastard. At least Hammy left with me, even if he was following the burger box. I blinked away angry tears. What a swine, leading me on when his ex-wife waited at home for him, presumably to reconcile.

Drew

It was time to pick up Gwen for the hospital visit, so I called in to Well Cottage on my way, hoping to explain. I knocked, but there was no reply. I was almost certain Hamburger whined once, but Amy

178

didn't respond. After last night and this morning, I could hardly blame her. Should I put a note through the door or try later? Better face to face, I decided.

I drove to Gwen's; to my father's old and it would appear, current girlfriend, my head buzzing. Women!

Gwen appeared to be as anxious as the last time I collected her.

'I'm sure Dad is out of danger,' I said. 'Although how we will manage when he comes out of the hospital, I've no idea. I'll have to work from home for a few weeks.'

'That's all sorted,' she said. 'He's going to stay with me as soon as he's fit for discharge. He'll use a walker for two days and then rely on the weight bearing plaster.'

'What? Are you certain you will manage?'

'I was a nurse for thirty years, for goodness' sake. Raymond said he'll pay Selwyn to look after the sheep, so you can get back to London.'

What should I say? I wondered. 'Um.., Thank you. Have to admit it would help, but aren't you rushing things?'

'We've missed nearly forty years of our lives, Drew. I don't want to miss any more. That's what I told him when I offered. Only…'

'Only?'

Her eyes screwed tight shut. 'There's one thing I haven't told him. Something important that might make him change his mind.'

'What?'

'I have to tell him first, then you need to know about it too.'

I dropped Gwen off at the hospital and contemplated going to Mum's. No, I'd ring the office check in there and then buy flowers for Amy. Something to make amends.

I rang Angel. 'Andrew, how are you? We've all been worrying about your father. How is he?'

'Sorry, I should have contacted you sooner. He's doing well. Out of intensive care and comfortable on the orthopaedic ward. He should be home soon. Thanks for asking.'

'Excellent news. I'll let the team know; we've all been thinking of you. Sally has asked to speak as soon as possible and I've blocked most calls. There was one strange one, though.'

'Oh?'

'A woman rang and demanded your number. She said she was your wife. I refused to give it out, said you were a divorcé. Anyway, if she'd been your wife, she'd already have your number.'

'Ah, I suspect it was my ex-wife. You did absolutely the right thing, Angel. Book me a call tomorrow with Daniel Kelly, will you? I'd like to check on the Helsinki project.'

'Of course, he's arranged a site visit later in the week.' She gulped and hesitated.

'And?' I asked. 'No problems with the project, I hope?'

'No, it's, um, I'm going with him. I haven't had a chance to ask for time off. Sally Gardner signed my leave sheet.' She rushed the words out as if dreading my response.

I had to laugh. 'I hope you have a great time. Finland's expensive; I'll pick up the tab for a fancy meal out for two. You both deserve it.'

'Thank you, so much. Should I connect you to Sally?'

Sally asked about Dad and then said, 'Drew, Stephanie was in touch last week asking to speak to you. Angelique put her through to me. Your ex-wife wanted her job back.'

'What?'

'I told her it wasn't appropriate, given the divorce. She told me she'd see about that and slammed the phone down.'

'I'm not amazed. You won't credit it, Steph came to Dad's yesterday. Drove all the way to Wales. Tried her old tricks and implied she'd like to try again.'

'Oh no! Drew, what did you say?'

'I sent her packing, of course. Saw through her wiles. You'd have been proud of me, Sal.'

'Thank goodness. After the call I did some digging in the US. Seems her contract wasn't renewed. Her new man has gone back to his wife and children. As Stephanie was on a probationary contract, the company declined to renew it.

'She'd be furious at that.'

'My guess is, word was out about her. That she's a man-eater and couldn't find anywhere else. The US firm wanted to employ you, originally. They only took her because they hoped it would persuade you to join their company.'

'Wow. Everything fits together now. I was a backup. A sucker.'

'I wouldn't go that far, Drew. I told you she'd regret leaving.'

'Huh, I would. I've learnt my lesson. Beware a wolf in cashmere goat clothing, eh?'

When we discussed my compassionate leave, I explained not as much time as I'd originally expected would be needed and promised to firm things up as soon as possible.

I considered my bigger problem; Amy. However could I make things right with her? In a florist near the hospital, I looked at expensive bunches of hothouse roses and orchids in glass jars. What Steph would have expected after a row. They didn't seem right. The shop overflowed with Christmas plants; poinsettias and bunches of dried flowers sprayed gold. They wouldn't work either, not romantic enough.

I spotted a basket of Paper Whites, scented narcissi; that seemed more Amy, but it was small. I needed more. Chocolates, a six-pack of beef burgers for Hammy? Ah, I'd go to Waitrose, and buy a bumper pack of vegetarian treats, with a cookbook. Mum loved the Christmas hamper I'd bought her last year.

I enjoyed myself, loading up a trolly with fruit and veg along with vegetarian mince pies, puddings, rose and violet chocolate creams, a Santa dog toy and at the last minute, a festive candle in a jar that had LED lights in gel around the edge. Women love fairy lights and it was Christmas soon. I hoped it would be enough. After the archeology fiasco, then Steph, I had to prove I wasn't an ogre or a philanderer.

On the ward, Gwen was still holding Dad's hand. I realised they were both red eyed. Had they been crying?

'How are you Dad?'

'I'm… I'm all right, adjusting to, to everything.' He looked at Gwen, who shook her head as if to say no.

'The good news is they'll let me come out tomorrow. They need the bed. The ward is full of broken hips. They say it's like that every time it snows. People go out, slip, fall and fracture. The nurses dread this weather.'

'And you're coming home?' I checked, uncertain that he'd really agreed to go to Gwen's.

'No, I'm going to Gwen's to recuperate. Once the fracture has mended, we'll go away. Somewhere warm, a cruise. Pick up a passport form for me in the post office, would you?'

At that, my jaw dropped open. 'You haven't taken a holiday in years; always insisted you couldn't leave the animals.'

He looked embarrassed. 'Travelling alone is no fun. Gwen wants to show me Hong Kong and its islands. I plan to spend your inheritance.'

'Dad, you can easily afford it. I've said you should travel for years. Offered to go with you. It's great and I'm pleased for you both.'

The two smiled, but I detected sadness in their expressions. Gwen's eyes were definitely red from crying. On the drive home to Talwern, Gwen sat silent. The atmosphere in the car was strange. I couldn't decide whether Gwen was afraid or about to cry.

As we approached the Storey Arms car park in the Beacons, she said, 'Drew, pull in please. I've something to tell you. Better that you're not driving. I've told your father, but it affects you as well. I hope to find it easier here, looking out at the view.'

I did as instructed. I wondered whatever this woman, a stranger for so many years, needed to tell me. It sounded as if she didn't want to look me in the eye.

'There's no easy way to say this, Drew. It's a secret I've kept since I was eighteen. I left Talwern and home because I was pregnant, pregnant with your father's child.'

She stopped, silent tears dripped down her cheeks.

'Gwen, I'm sorry.'

'You are the last person who needs to apologise, Drew. I do and maybe your father, but not you.'

I had meant I was sorry for her, not apologise, but didn't correct her.

'Did you have a termination? That must have been dreadful.'

'No, I had the baby. You have a half-brother, Drew. I called him Paul, but who knows what his adoptive parents called him.'

'I have another brother? A half-brother? My goodness.' I struggled with the idea, then asked, 'Did Dad know about the pregnancy?'

'I didn't tell him. My parents sent me away to a Catholic home for unmarried mothers. When he didn't write, I was too proud to let him know.

'Raymond told me he sent letter after letter for weeks after I left. My parents told him I'd a new boyfriend and didn't want him to have my address. They promised to forward his letters. But of course, they never did.'

'Oh Gwen, what a terrible thing to discover. I suppose Dad turned to my mother because of that. They always told me they had a rebound relationship. Warned me to take my time finding the right woman.'

'Yes. I'm sorry that you never knew you have a brother.'

'But if you hadn't left, I wouldn't be here. I'm not sure it is possible for me to regret what happened.'

Gwen appeared taken aback. 'I've never considered that. You are the one person who wouldn't.'

My emotions were confused; sad for Dad and Gwen, but aware that if they had not separated, I'd not have been born.

'Have you traced him? Paul I mean?'

'I tried twenty years ago, but got nowhere. I'd hoped he'd contact me. Your father thinks we should try again, that things may have changed with agencies now.'

I sighed. 'It's going to take time to adjust to the news. Let's speak again tomorrow, after Dad settles into your place. Do you need me to shift furniture? I'll help any way I can.'

She nodded, then apologised again. As she got out of the car, she said, 'Amy knows about Paul. She is the only person I ever told. Telling her made it easier with your father.'

Chapter 19

Amy

A knock sounded at the front door next morning and Drew's car was stopped outside the gate. Eyes puffy, nose red and swollen after my tears, I looked a fright. Why was that bloody man bothering me again?

I ignored his knock. What was the point? The man led me on last night. Made me believe he was different, trustworthy, but let me down, again. I'd given him a second chance. How wrong could I have been? That woman, his ex, was gorgeous, and they'd spent the night in Rooks Row together.

I'd pretend to be out, give myself a few days, then tell him exactly what I thought of him. How dare he treat me like that? Hammy yapped and made for the door and I pulled him back by his collar. Hopefully, Drew wouldn't have heard.

An hour later, the knocker sounded again. Damn, Andrew Giles. Why was he still bothering me? Face fierce, I flung the door open to give him a piece of my mind.

I'm not sure whether Ben or I were more surprised at the thud as the door bounced on its hinges.

'Hi Amy… Sorry to bother you. I, um, hoped for a chat,' he said.

'Ben. Sorry. I thought you were… Of course, come in. Verity said that you'd gone to your Mum's…'

'You've seen her then?'

'Yes.'

'How is she?'

'Distraught, in a proper state when I saw her yesterday.'

I was unsure how much to tell him, wanted to feel my way.

He ran a hand through his hair, looked at his boots, then said, 'I drove back to see the kids. We can't leave them wondering, not knowing where I am, after hearing us argue like that.'

'Mmm, you're right.'

'I wanted to see Vee, too. Kept wondering how she was doing. I'm confused and feel betrayed.'

I couldn't stop myself. I said, 'Join the club.'

He didn't acknowledge that, simply continued. 'I thought Simon was my mate. It's been hard moving here. All of us having to make new friends, the kids, Vee. When we met someone as interested in music as Verity and a laugh, it was great.'

'Then she told me they'd had an affair. Said she regretted it, that it was a mistake and she's been a fool. I didn't know what to think. Hard to get my head around it. To make it worse, a few hours later, Simon called. I'd garaged the car, and he didn't realise I'd come home.'

He stopped, gazed at me in pain, then continued, 'I... I confronted him. He had the cheek to tell me it was Vee's imagination; a fantasy. That she chased him. I may have been blind, but I'm not bloody stupid. Anyway, one thing led to another, and we scrapped. The kids must have heard it all. It will have scared them.'

'He called here afterwards and tried to pretend he'd fallen off his motorbike. You gave him a pasting,' I said.

'Bastard.'

'Turns out that is Simon's reputation locally,' I said. 'As outsiders, we couldn't have known.'

He raked his hair with his hand again.

'I love Verity and we've two children together. It's a disaster. What should I do?'

'Ben, I'm the last person to ask for advice. I've messed up every relationship I've ever had. For what it's worth, Simon totally fooled me, too. Initially, I thought he was interested in me, that we might make a go of it. I started having doubts a while back. Not because of Verity, more that he asked nothing about me. Everything referred to himself.'

Ben nodded. 'You're right. Even with Vee, he only took an interest when he found out about her Royal College of Music background. Her teaching there, and the albums she's played on. Before that, he pretty much ignored her.'

'Typical narcissist,' I said. 'The penny dropped for me weeks ago. But he can be charming and Vee was —'

'Lonely,' Ben finished my phrase.

'You should go home, talk to her. Verity said she can't imagine life without you.'

He gave a weak smile. 'I will… I'm not sure. Trust's a funny thing, isn't it?'

As Ben drove off, I pondered his comment. Did I trust Drew? He'd told me that conditions were too icy for his ex-wife to drive to London last night. That certainly was true. Maybe the rest of his explanation was too? Everything Mr Giles had told me about her suggested she was difficult to say the least. I'd disliked her on sight.

I want back to work on the laptop all afternoon, envious of the blue skies behind my colleagues in a Zoom call to Melbourne, but thoughts about Drew intruded constantly.

A text pinged through at three; Gwen.

'Told Raymond. Went OK, not angry. Will tell Andrew on the way back.'

Gosh, how would Drew react to knowing about a brother he'd never heard of?

At five, the knocker sounded yet again. As I peered out of the window, there was the familiar shape of Drew's car at the gate. I wasn't ready to see him and needed time. He called through the letterbox. How long would he stay out there? I wondered. Should I relent? He'd had a tough day. Hammy barked enthusiastically; he liked Drew.

The knocking stopped, but the car didn't leave. Footsteps trudged, crunching through a snowdrift, and made for the shed. I watched him pick up Jen's ladder and carry it towards the side of the house, to the bathroom window.

Idiot. Didn't he know how slippery the frozen rungs would be? He mustn't try to climb through. Suppose he fell? I rushed out of the back door. He had reached the top.

What should I do? I put a foot on the bottom rung and called out to him stop?

He twisted, the ladder wobbled as he put out a leg to climb through. A rip appeared in his jeans.

I had to stop myself from laughing and told him to come down.

I had to say it. 'Showing off your drawers again. My gran warned me not to show anyone my underwear if I wanted to be respected.'

He let out a guffaw and descended. When he reached the ground, I worked out why they'd torn. He was wearing the tightest pair of jeans imaginable, his flesh bulged over the waistband. Goodness, what had got into him?

'I um...'

'Oh, come in out of the cold. Sit down and hide your shame. I'll make us a cup of tea,'I said.

'Wait a sec.'

He disappeared briefly, then returned carrying two baskets. One held narcissi, my favourite scented variety and an interesting-looking hamper.

He gazed at me, voice plaintive, 'I needed to make amends, apologise as well as thanking you, for, well, for everything. I'm sorry for calling Hamburger Jet, for not trusting you or the dog; and that I was rude about archeologists. Thank you for befriending Dad, for saving his life and for braving the storm to stop the sheep from freezing.'

I nodded. He was right, I damn well deserved thanking, so did Hammy.

He stepped towards me, expression serious. 'I didn't even know that my ex-wife was in the UK, let along planning to visit, and made her leave as soon as it was safe. I realise what she implied by talking about the bed being comfortable. That's how she behaves, but there wasn't a scrap of truth in it.'

I nodded a second time, my eyes felt sore, as if I might cry. I believed Drew and trusted him.

'Can we take up where we left off last night?' he asked.

I nodded a third time, then stepped into his arms.

Drew

When I returned to Rooks Row, the need to see Amy, to hold her and explain, overwhelmed me. I wanted to discuss what Gwen's bombshell, but mostly to look at her sweet face. Explain about Stephanie. Wipe away the hurt look from the morning.

I looked at my old cords. Stephanie's barb stung; I had let things slide these last few months. A pair of old jeans from my trainee days languished at the back of the wardrobe, so I dug them out. I hadn't worn those Wrangler jeans in what, fifteen years? Pale denim and straight cut; back in fashion, I reassured myself. Less, what had Stephanie said, "Grandad chic." I pulled them on with difficulty. Much tighter than I remembered, they pinched in the worst possible places as I bent to pick up the flower basket, balanced it on the hamper. I trudged through the snow and up the lane to Well Cottage.

My stomach churned as I walked up the path to Amy's and knocked. The dog whined, but no one came. She wouldn't let me in.

191

I called through the letterbox. 'Amy, It's Drew. Please open the door. Give me a chance to explain.'

Nothing, silence. The door remained closed.

I tried again. Damn it; she had to listen. Should I leave the flowers on the doorstep? No, I wanted to see her, needed to hold her. Explain and talk about what Gwen had told me. I looked up. The bathroom window was open.

I'd got in that way before and could do it again. Amy had to listen.

What if she called the police? It was entering without permission. I brushed the thought away, simply had to see her.

As I extracted the ladder from the hooks outside the shed, a face appeared at the kitchen window; Amy. I carried it round, pushed it firmly into place, took off my jacket and climbed. Icy cold rungs burnt my hands.

At the top, I stretched a leg towards the window. Amy stood below me, stamping in the snow.

'What on earth are you doing?' she shouted.

I looked down. The ladder wobbled wildly. I reached over to the windowsill to stop it tipping, only to hear a ripping noise; my jeans.

'Oh, for goodness' sake, come down and take care.' She giggled, cheeks rosy in the cold.

My hand went to my jeans. A six-inch tear in the rear displayed my underpants; again.

'I had to see you, to explain,' I said.

I was so grateful to those old Wrangler jeans. If they hadn't ripped and made her laugh, I'm not sure she'd have relented. Seeing her smiling up at me made my heart skip a beat. Then she stepped into my arms and tilted her head up to be kissed, once I put my lips to hers I couldn't stop. Kiss dissolved into kiss. Each breath felt ragged, it was all I could do not drag her into the cottage.

I pulled myself together, forced myself to stop. Dad's words "don't mess it up" rang in my ears.

'I've brought you something.' I hurried to the front door and returned with the flowers and hamper.

'Paper whites, my favourite narcissi, bring them in.'

Hamburger lay curled by her log burner. He looked up, wagged his tail half-heartedly and drifted back into a doze. My senses jolted. This was what it felt like to come home, somewhere warm and welcoming. Sleek and sophisticated was OK, but who wanted that when you could be safe, loved and cosy?

'Tea, coffee?'

'No, just this,' I said and began to kiss her again.

Later she asked. 'So your car's in the farmyard?'

I nodded.

'And your father's not home. Soo.'

'So?'

'So you don't have to leave? The village grapevine will have no way of knowing you're here.'

She leant forward and gave me a long, tantalising kiss, deep and intense, her tongue flickering around my lips.

I gave up; pulled her toward me and explored every part of her face, lips, cheeks, earlobes, and unbuttoned her blouse. This couldn't be messing up; it felt so right.

Chapter 20

Amy

I woke at seven enveloped in Drew's arms. It felt like heaven. Already awake, he watched me, head propped on one arm. I gave what I hoped was a sexy smile, then bent forward to let my mouth linger on his as he caressed my back.

At eight, Gwen rang.

'Um, is Andrew with you, by any chance?'

'He is. How did you…?'

'He wasn't in Rooks Row when I called, and I rather thought… Oh Amy, his father says he's been moping after you for months.'

'Really?'

'Yes. Anyway, can I speak to him? I need help to move a bed downstairs for when Raymond comes. He won't make the stairs with a fractured leg.'

'Here he is.' I raised my eyebrows at Drew, and mouthed the word 'Gwen,' handed over the phone and nestled onto his chest to listen.

'We'll be with you in about an hour or so,' he said. 'Are you sure about taking Dad in? It's a lot to ask of anyone,' he said.

'I've never been more certain of anything for years,' Gwen said.

He put the phone on the bedside table, stroked my face, and smiled. We've two hours before getting to Gwen's. 'How will we spend the time?'

'Oh, I guess you'll think of something.'

We were late reaching Gwen's, partly because Drew went to Rooks Row and retrieve an intact pair of trousers and muttered about needing to check his old emails.Dismantling, then moving a double bed and mattress down the ancient dark oak staircase and into Gwen's sitting room was hard work.

As I helped make up the bed, she tutted. 'That is hopeless. Duvets and fitted sheets, have destroyed a nation's ability to make a bed. I'll show you how make a hospital corner.'

All three of us had built up a sweat by the time the room was ready.

'I've coffee cake in the tin,' Gwen said. 'We deserve a slice each.'

As we sat, Drew cleared his throat. 'When you told me about my half-brother, something niggled at my memory.'

Gwen stilled. He extracted a sheet of printer paper from his pocket.

'A couple of years ago, my mother started researching her family history. She took one of those DNA tests. Last Christmas, she gave my brother, sister and me kits to do the same. To keep her happy, each of us gave saliva samples. Mum managed the accounts and traced our different trees back.

'There are message boards on the Ancestry site, and one day Mum forwarded me an odd message from someone called Francis. It said he'd been adopted as a baby, and that DNA suggested he and I had a very close relationship on our father's side. He asked me to contact him.'

One of Gwen's hands covered her mouth, the other clutched at my arm.

'I presumed it was a scam. We are a small family. There is no possibility of even a cousin on Dad's side and didn't reply. I discussed the message with my mum; we were perplexed. The DNA gave an exceptionally close match, a first cousin, or closer. Mum said that DNA couldn't lie. I agreed, but also thought sample mix ups must happen. I didn't mentioned it to Dad, but it has bothered me ever since.'

Gwen stared at me. 'Do you think?' she whispered. 'Is it possible?'

Drew replied, 'Honestly, it's more than possible. It was almost certainly him.'

He held out the sheet with the email address to her.

She read the email slowly. 'I don't know what to do, what to say. Can I talk it through with Raymond? Francis, he's called Francis, the same as my grandfather. He may hate me. Do you think that's why he contacted you but never tried to find me?'

Drew dodged the question. 'Francis might have changed his email address, since last year, or it could be a scam.'

His mobile rang, making all three of us jump. It was the hospital, asking whether arrangements were in place for Raymond's discharge. Desperate for beds, they told us a Powys ambulance was at A&E and would return empty unless he used it.

Gwen rushed to make lunch and asked Drew to stay to help settle his father in.

I checked my phone. I'd two texts from Verity, who wanted me to go round that afternoon. Leaving them space to sort out Mr Giles over the next few hours seemed a good idea. I told Drew where I was off.

'See you later. Um, your place or mine?' He pulled me to him with a wicked grin. 'Not that it matters; my plans for either are the same.'

I blinked slowly up at him and tried to look innocent. 'What can you mean? I'll meet you back in Well Cottage at six. Don't wear last night's jeans. You wouldn't want to shock my gran.'

He grinned, amused eyes meeting mine. 'I rather think I might. See you at six.'

When I reached the Oaks, Ben's car was parked up in the drive. The children were building a snowman outside, little Wilf bounded round them, barely visible in the thick snow, yapping with joy.

Ben welcomed me in with a hug. 'Hi, Amy. Vee's upstairs, I'll call her. Go into the conservatory. I'll make you girls tea.'

Tea, it was the first time for ages I hadn't been offered wine at The Oaks.

Vee looked tired, drawn and thin when she joined me. 'Hi Amy, we're glad you came. I wanted to update you on everything. You've been so good.' She picked at her nails.

'Thank you for sending Ben home. Telling him I loved him and couldn't imagine life without him. It made a difference.'

197

Ben brought in the tea tray then left, saying he'd go to play with the kids.

Verity's face tensed. 'It's a relief to talk to someone who knows. Ben has taken me back. We're going to try again, but will leave Talwern and make a fresh start. We'll find somewhere outside London, close enough to be commutable for Ben, so I'm not alone as much.'

'I will play with my old band while Ben babysits and go back to recording sessions. Carry on my music career.' Vee took a breath. 'I've stopped drinking; it didn't help.' She smiled thoughtfully. 'This house is gorgeous and so is the village, but a home is more than a house. It needs two people working together, bringing up a family.'

'I'll miss you.'

'I'll miss you too. When we find somewhere, you must come and stay.'

'I will, but I may need to bring someone.' Verity's face reflected panic.

'No, not Simon; as if! It's Andrew Giles. We've sort of got together. This time, I really believe it will work. He's the one. I've never felt like this about anyone before.'

'Andrew Giles, goodness.' She looked thoughtful for a moment. 'Not your usual type, but maybe it's about time. The usual type never worked out for you, did they?'

Chapter 21

Drew

On Monday Amy woke me as she crept out of bed at ten to seven. I stretched out a hand and grabbed her wrist.

'I warned you. I've a meeting booked with Melbourne,' she said.

'One last cwtch.'

Cwtch?

'Cuddle in Welsh,' I pulled her warm body back to me.

'Drew, no, I have to be dressed, made up. I'll bring you up a coffee.'

Reluctantly, I released my grip. Ten minutes later, the smell of fresh coffee roused me from my doze.

'What will you do today?' Amy asked.

'Check in on Dad at Gwen's first. She may have realised how difficult he can be by now, and want him gone. Then I'll catch up with the office. I have to go to London for meetings early tomorrow morning but I'll be back on Friday , Office will close for the holidays then.'

Amy smiled. 'Gwen won't take any nonsense from your dad. If it comes to a battle of wills, I know who my money's on. It's not your father.'

'You've no idea how cantankerous and stubborn he is.'

'He won't stand a chance. She ran a hospital for years, remember and will have his measure. May not need it, of course. Your Dad is smitten.'

I gazed up at her, 'So am I.'

Her eyes softened. 'Me too. See you after work then. Is seven OK? I've got another intercontinental Zoom meeting scheduled. I'll take Hammy for a run at lunchtime.'

I reached Gwen's at eight-thirty. Dad sat up in a chair, neatly dressed, hair combed with his leg elevated by two pillows. He was dipping bread soldiers into a boiled egg, while Gwen dusted furniture around him.

She stopped as I entered, removed the sheet of paper with Francis's email from her pocket, and held it out to me.

'We talked this over last night, Andrew and concluded that since Francis emailed you, it was best if you replied. Would you ask him if he'd meet us?'

'Sure, when I know more, I'll tell you at once.'

Their faces reflected a mixture of relief and fear. If Francis agreed to see them, what would this stranger be like?

Back in Rooks Row, I drafted a cautious email from my personal account; writing and re-writing phrases to the brother I'd never met. The email was formal, probably too formal.

Dear Francis,

I must apologise for not replying sooner. There are no close relatives on my father's side of the family at all, so your message confused me. My grandfather's

*only brother died in the war, my dad is an only child.
After he suffered a serious accident, we discovered
that I have a half-brother, adopted months before I was
born. The DNA results suggest you may be that
brother.*

*I wondered whether you would like to meet up? I'm
not sure where you live and when might be a good
time?*

Andrew Giles.

I pressed send with trepidation. A brother; what
would he be like? I'd never experienced an absence of
siblings; my little sister and stepfather's son filled that
space. The same as so many kids in school with
divorced parents, I'd visited Dad every other weekend.
It had been a pain coming to Talwern in later years. I'd
have preferred to go out with my friends, meet girls. I
always went though, knew how much Dad valued our
spending time together.

The morning passed with my replying to queries
from work and day dreaming. As I'd watched Amy
wake earlier, a lump had formed in my throat. So this
was what love was like? Someone to take your breath
away, to hold tight and close, no barriers.

At half five I logged out and checked my personal
emails. There was a reply from Francis. It was equally
formal and guarded. I chuckled, thinking I could have
written it myself.

Dear Andrew,

Thank you for your email. It was unexpected and I'm torn how to respond. When I contacted you, I had recently discovered my adoption; months later my life and emotions have settled. It appears my birth father is still alive and I'm glad of that. I live and work in St Albans. If you are ever in London, you and I could meet for a coffee? I'd prefer not to see any other family members.

Francis

No surname, that was interesting; he didn't want anyone searching for him, or turning up unannounced.

In response I wrote;

Dear Francis,

I entirely understand. Neither my father nor I had any idea that you existed until a few days ago. To say this has come as a shock is an understatement. Both of your natural parents are alive. They asked me to say they would love to meet, but appreciate you may not be ready.

A coffee sounds an excellent way forward. I work in London, and will be in town later in the week. Other than Friday, any late afternoon slot would be suitable. I suggest Rails bar at St Pancras station. How would 4pm on Thursday suit?

Andrew

He replied minutes later, agreeing the time. I printed out his email to show Gwen and Dad that evening.

Gwen was bitterly disappointed when I went round. 'He doesn't sound enthusiastic, does he? He's implying he was prepared to meet when he first found out, but not now.' She sighed, 'I can't blame him, it will have been hard discovering someone gave you away at birth.'

The following Wednesday, I took the tube to St Pancras. The Christmas crowd meant it was full of parties. In the corner of the bar, reading a newspaper, sat a man whose face I half recognised. It had to be Francis.

I introduced myself. As he stood we stared at each other. We were the same height with similar hair and eyes. I wondered what to say? What do you do when meeting a half-brother for the first time? Should we hug? Do the kiss on the cheek thing? He extended his hand for me to shake; what a relief.

'Andrew, good to meet you.'

'Likewise, I've been trying to work out why I knew it was you. It's because you resemble my grandfather. Younger than when I knew him, but you're very similar.'

'Am I? It sounds strange you saying that. For years, people said how much I look like my adoptive father. And I do, it just turns out we were never blood relations.' He raised a quizzical eyebrow, then rubbed his lips before speaking. Taking his time, exactly the way my grandfather used to. It was uncanny.

'I expect you're wondering how I found out?' he asked. 'My parents,' he paused, 'my proper parents, the people who raised me, never told me. I discovered my adoption a year ago.'

'What happened?'

'I needed my degree certificate when I applied for an Open University course. Mum and Dad were watching Strictly Come Dancing on TV when I called. Not wanting to disturb them, I went to the desk where they keep all that admin stuff.'

He rubbed his mouth again and I realised how painful this was for him.

'Next to my degree certificate was an envelope labelled birth certificates. I'd never needed mine. My parents got me my first passport when I was ten, used it at that time, I imagine. I'd no call for it since; a passport is proof enough of identity and you send it off to renew it.

'Out of curiosity I glanced at Mum's certificate then realised my birth certificate looked different. I saw the words, "Date of adoption order," printed on it.'

He swallowed, then sighed. 'I put it back in the envelope, found the degree certificate and left. It took me a while to begin to comprehend what I'd discovered.'

After a pause he said, 'I have asked nothing about you, Drew. Sorry, I'm being rude. This isn't all about me. Tell me about yourself. How you found out.'

I outlined Dad's fall and the subsequent reconciliation with his first love, Gwen. That it had been a teenage romance, and how young they were. 'Gwen and her family kept it a secret. Dad didn't know, and met someone else soon after, my mother. They had to marry; Mum was pregnant. You're seven months older than me.'

'Good breeding stock, your dad,' Francis joked. He corrected himself. 'Our father, I should say.'

I explained about my parent's divorce, and that I'd been happy with my step-family.

'I expected your Welsh accent. The DNA test shows most of my ancestors are from Wales and the borders.'

'Near Brecon, both families come from a small village a few miles outside the town, farming stock,'I replied.

'I've no brothers and sisters. When I finally plucked up the courage to ask my parents, they were ashamed. They'd meant to tell me when I was eighteen, but couldn't bear to. Said I was completely theirs as far as they were concerned, never regarded me as anything else. They'd raised me since I was six weeks old, after all. Everyone comments about how much I look like them. I couldn't have had better parents, nor my children, better grandparents.'

'You're married then; not divorced like Dad and me?'

'Happily married, we've been together for sixteen years. Why do you ask ?'

'Dad has always said Giles men are hopeless with women, unlucky in love. I sort of expect my relationships to fail.'

'Sounds to me like his girlfriend running off at eighteen scarred him badly. That is his problem and his life, not yours. You are responsible for your own screw-ups in my book. Success with relationships is not predestined, they take love, work, and a little luck.'

'Maybe...' I pondered. He was right. No one made me duck out of commitment every time a woman got close to me. Stephanie ignored my reticence, and carried on regardless, but I hadn't loved her. I'd always buried my emotions to protect myself from being hurt the way Dad had been. It had taken Amy to change that. I'd never felt remotely the same about anyone as I did about her.

'You said you have children? Do I have more nieces and nephews?' I asked.

'Two; here, see.' He took out his wallet and extracted a photo of a cheerful family standing by a pond. His wife stood beside a tall girl, entering adolescence, and a laughing boy.

Francis said, 'I decided not to trace or contact my birth mother; didn't see any benefit. She'd abandoned me and it would upset everyone I love, but.'

'But?'

'But I couldn't stop wondering. It eats at you, knowing you've been given away. Why, why would someone do that to a baby? I took the DNA test, half hoping it wouldn't find a match and half hoping it would.'

'Gwen, your birth mother said she thinks about you every day. How you looked in her arms a baby. She never married or had children. She was eighteen and sitting her A-Levels when her parents made her give you up.'

He shrugged, 'Poor girl. I'd guessed at something like that. Even so, my life is settled. I don't need new parents.' His voice broke. 'Give them this photo, and tell her; my mother I mean, she did the right thing. That I had a great upbringing.'

He stood to leave. 'I'll email you. I always dreamt about having a brother as a kid. Someone to kick a ball around with. It's lonely being an only child.'

'It'd be good to meet up again, whatever. Take your time. I respect what you're saying. What do you do for a living, by the way? They're bound to ask.'

'I'm a vet.'

The office shut for the fortnight's Christmas break on Friday lunchtime. Everyone would work from home over the next few days. Most of the staff headed to the pub, but I was keen to get away and miss the worst of the motorway traffic and gave apologies. Before she left, I gave Angel her usual bottle of perfume and asked about her plans.

'I'm going to Ireland to meet Daniel's parents for a few days before Christmas. I can't wait, it sounds lovely on the West coast. How about you? Any plans with the girl in the village you keep mentioning? Amy, the one with the dog?'

'Do I keep mentioning her? I hadn't realised. He's my dog though. Although, Hammy acts like he's hers.' I found myself grinning inanely just thinking about Amy.

'Andrew, the entire office has heard all about her.' Angel's eyes danced with mirth. 'You say her name whenever you can. You're besotted.'

I called at Gwen's on the way back. Dad sat on a chair in her kitchen, sharpening a set of chisels. They gave a gentle shink, shink as he smoothed their edges on the oily grey whetstone.

'Dad, I was thinking.' I stopped trying to find the right words, not give too much away.

'Yes, you usually are. What do you want?'

'Grandma's old posy ring; the family one...'

'The one that is engraved inside with "Trew Love is my Desyre," you mean?'

'Is that what it says? I'd forgotten.'

'Had you? Well, it does; and it would make a lovely Christmas present should anyone need a ring as a gift. Especially for the sort of girl who's into old things.'

We both laughed.

'The ring's in the jewellery box under my bed, beneath the loose floorboard. Your grandmother's diamond engagement ring is in there as well as a matter of fact. I agree that the posy ring would make a lovely Christmas present for Amy, just right for her.'

'I thought that, too. Thanks, Dad.'

'I'm pleased. I like Amy. I was relieved when you didn't ask for either ring for that woman you married. I'd have refused.'

He still couldn't bring himself to say Steph's name. He made a fair point; she'd have sold or remodelled them. I'd never considered giving the family pieces to her, or dared mention they existed.

Chapter 22

Amy

A few days later, I was having a coffee at Gwen's when the topic of Christmas Day came up. Mr Giles, who I was slowly learning to call Raymond, said, 'Drew and I will spend Christmas with Gwen, but what are you doing? Your parents are in New Zealand.'

'I've planned a quiet day in front of the TV. Mum's sister invited me to stay with them in Birmingham. With my cousins and my Gran there, it'll be too much. I had an early Christmas with my parents before they left, so I'll visit my grandmother for the New Year. I've an interview to prep for anyway.'

'Nonsense, you must join us here. In fact, please stay for a couple of nights, so you don't need to drive in the morning,' said Gwen. She coughed. 'It's a big house, six bedrooms, so there is plenty of privacy.' She winked at Raymond after she'd said privacy and I gave an internal sigh. The village grapevine; they'd been told where Drew was spending his nights.

Gwen continued, 'It'll be lovely having people, family here, like old times. I usually hate Christmas.' Her eyes misted over. She was thinking of Francis. When Drew told her Francis didn't feel able to see her or commit to meeting she'd been devastated.

Raymond interrupted and said, 'Go up to the orchard tomorrow and pick a pile of mistletoe; some for the shop and some for here. We're having a tree delivered tomorrow. Drew will help set it upright; I'm useless with this leg. Gwen and I will put up decorations together. Come round and see it after supper.'

'I'll have hot mince pies ready,' said Gwen.

Drew and I discussed staying over at Gwen's that evening. He shook his head and gave a wicked grin. 'Let's only stay for Christmas night. I've other plans for Christmas Eve; come to that, I've plans for tonight too. Where's that mistletoe you picked earlier?'

'My gran would say,"Enough is as good as a feast."'

'I'm going to have to meet your gran,' he laughed.

How serious were we? I wondered. Would he commit to meeting my family? I knew his father obviously, but he'd never mentioned taking me to see his mother in Cardiff.

'You could come with me when I go at New Year? It won't be exciting. We stay in and watch fireworks from her bedroom window at midnight. She's eighty-five and doesn't enjoy being out late, but she'd like to meet you.'

'If you're there, it will be excitement enough; and your grandmother sounds a real character.'

'She is. I hope I get the County archeology job or else…'

'Or else?'

'If I don't I'm homeless again. I guess I'll ought to at least try Australia. It'd be madness to buy a house in the UK right now. I would miss my Gran and my parents, as well as all my new friends in Talwern so much though.'

I wasn't sure if I imagined Drew's face pale. He was quiet for the rest of the evening.

We had a blissful time over the next two days, took long walks with Hammy spending the days and nights together.

Christmas Eve morning, he checked his emails sitting at the central kitchen island in Rooks Row as I made a vegetarian festive roast loaf to take to Gwen's.

'Read this. We'll have to go to Gwen's tonight after all,' he said, pushing his laptop towards me.

Dear Andrew,

I haven't been able to get meeting you and the story of why I was adopted and learning how young my birth mother was, out of my head. She was only six years older than my daughter and must have felt abandoned and desperate when my grandparents sent her away pregnant at eighteen. I discussed everything with my parents. Mum was worried they'd lose me, but Dad insisted that meeting them was the right thing to do. He said otherwise I'd always wonder otherwise, especially if something happened to one of them. After what you told me about our father nearly dying in the snow, I decided he was right.

As a first step, I wondered whether we could Zoom tonight? Would six o'clock suit? I'd say hello and wish

them Happy Christmas. If it goes OK, I will drive to
Wales and meet them in the New Year.
  Francis.

'Goodness, Gwen will be so pleased. What about your father? He hasn't said much, has he?'

' No, he's concerned I'll feel displaced and is insisting on going to our solicitors. Want to make over Rooks Row to me after Christmas. He says he will be staying at Gwen's and is not certain he'll ever move home. They're planning a joint venture, a vineyard and have even got a name for the wine and designed a label. They'll call it Gwennol Winery. Gwennol means swallow in Welsh. A pun, I guess'

'And it combines Gwen's name. How romantic.'

'They're like twenty-year-olds planning a future together. Dad told me you only get one life and they want to live theirs together from now on. I told him I didn't mind sharing Rook's Row, if someone else has a right to it.' Drew's face shadowed.

'You do mind?'

'Honestly, yes I would have. I love the old place and always expected to end up there. Dad says Gwen's house and land will go to Francis. He will assure my interests, as well as avoid inheritance tax, by giving me the house. The accident made him consider what would happen if he died suddenly. He told me the thought of the taxman having the house kept him going when he was trapped under the tractor.'

'Shall we tell them about Francis' Zoom call or let it be a surprise?'

'We'll say we're calling in with a gift that needs to be opened at once. They'll assume it's food, something fresh.'

'OK, but Hamburger hasn't been out all day. Can we walk with him? It's a lovely night and there'll be stars later?'

'You and that dog, I'm not sure if I should be pleased or jealous.'

I said, 'I guess I did fall in love with him first, you second,' then froze. Oh no, I'd used the L word and we'd only been properly together for just over a week. I'd rushed in again, probably ruined the whole thing. I glanced sideways. Drew hadn't noticed; was relaxed, and laughed at my response but didn't say he loved me back. He'd told me he was smitten, but what did that actually mean? That he fancied me? Lusted after me?

Early evening, we went into Gwen's sitting room, set up the computer on the coffee table, then sat them on the sofa in front of it. Gwen raised an eyebrow in query as Drew logged in and the beep beep of a Zoom call sounded.

'We're speaking to your parents and Jen in New Zealand. You're engaged! How wonderful,' she said.

'No, no, it's not...' I stammered, then blushed puce.

The beeping stopped as Francis picked up the call. His face gazed at us on the screen, and the colour drained from Gwen's face.

Francis smiled. 'Hello from St Albans,' he said. 'Happy Christmas.'

'Hello,' Gwen whispered back.

Raymond took her hand and nodded wordlessly at the son he'd not known existed until two weeks ago.

'Uh, how's the weather with you? It's chilly here,' Francis appeared as unsure what to say as they did.

A boy burst onto the screen, about eight, with unruly dark hair, he asked, 'Who are you talking to Dad?' Brown eyes like his grandfather and uncle's peered at us. 'Who are those people? Is that a dog? What's its name?'

I waited. Allowed his family to reply.

'He's called Hamburger,' Drew said and laughed.

'Is he a border collie? Can he herd sheep?'

'He can; especially when Amy gives the commands.' Drew took my hand. Francis nodded at me and said, 'Nice to meet you, Amy. Drew mentioned someone special, but not that you could herd sheep.'

The boy interrupted. 'Cool, I'd like to try shepherding. I watch it on Country File all the time.'

Raymond said, 'If you visit, I'll teach you.'

'Brilliant, I'll tell Sophie. She's my big sister.' He disappeared off the screen.

With a smile, Francis said, 'That ball of energy is David. You realise he'll nag me to death until I bring him to see your dog?'

Gwen had remained speechless, knuckles white as she held Raymond's hand, but finally gasped out, 'I'd love that. Love to meet all of you.'

The call ended after a few more minutes. Gwen smiled through tears of happiness. We made our excuses and left them to talk about the call.

The dark skies of Breconshire glittered with a million pinpoints of light as we walked with Hamburger back to Well Cottage.

Drew pulled me close to his side and asked, 'You know what Gwen thought at the beginning of the call?'

'Yes, I was so embarrassed, sorry.'

'I'm not. When you said you might leave and go to Australia two days ago, I couldn't stand it. Could barely breathe. I don't want you to leave. I know this is too soon. We've barely had a chance to get to know each other, but I've never felt like this about anyone before. I'm in love with you. Us together feels right, just wonderful. I'm hoping you feel the same.'

He fumbled in his pocket and produced a small leather box. 'This was going to be a Christmas present, but Dad is right. You only get one life; let's live it; together. Amy Stuart, wild, marrow exploding archeologist, would you consider marrying this pain of an architect?'

The End

If you enjoyed this novel, it would be great if you have time put up a review on Amazon. Getting ratings reviews makes a big difference to authors. Thanks

Acknowledgements

Yet again, I must thank my writing buddies, Sharif Gemie, Pamela Cartlidge from Cardiff Writers' Circle along with Sian Stewart, for generously giving their time to offer constructive comments as well as pointing out the numerous early typos.

I should also mention that a beautiful painting of Miss Jean Hayton, and its background inspired part of this story. Jean lived a long and happy life. I combined her story with the tragedy of my great aunt and her untimely death from TB. Lillie's fiancé returned from the war just before her death. He never married, telling people he could never find anyone to replace her. The Giles family are fictional.

There is a fantastic walk to the Wellington Bomber crash site as well as photos if you would like to retrace Amy's walk with the rambler group that is available on my website.

About the Author;

S. E. Morgan has published three previous historical fiction novels, two set in Victorian Wales;

From Waterloo to Water Street,
A Welsh Not
and one in 5th Century Ireland;
The King over the Sea

Printed in Great Britain
by Amazon